"So, Mr. Quarterback," Selena said unevenly, "do you have a name?"

He hesitated a second, seeming reluctant to tell her. "Trader," he answered finally.

"Trader," she repeated dreamily. "Trader what?"

"Just Trader. It's a nickname."

She lifted her drink approvingly. "Here's to you, Mr. Trader the Elderly Quarterback. May your second chance be a success."

"And to you, Selena Derringer," he added gallantly. "May you follow your star, wherever it may lead you."

Down went the drink, hitting her stomach like a bomb. Her mind began to fade in and out, and the last thing she remembered clearly was nestling against the shelter of his powerful chest, softly murmuring, "Touchdown, Trader. Touchdown..."

Diana Morgan

Diana Morgan is a pseudonym for a husband-and-wife team. They met at a phone booth at Columbia University, and have been together romantically and professionally ever since. They enjoy opera, pigging out, small children and elves (especially their daughter Elizabeth), their retreat in the Berkshires, and trying to figure out what will happen next on Hill Street Blues.

Other Second Chance at Love books by
Diana Morgan

ANYTHING GOES #286

Dear Reader:

Laine Allen, author of *Undercover Kisses* (#276), returns with another pair of beguiling lovers in *The Fire Within* (#304). Former nurse Cara Chandler loyally hopes to build a future on the bittersweet foundation of a lost love. Dynamo millionaire Lou Capelli dreams of finding a woman honest enough to gaze at him with love—not dollar signs—in her eyes. But the passion that melds them together just as cataclysmically tears them apart. A tender and tormenting love story . . .

Prolific Lee Williams brings us *Whispers of an Autumn Day* (#305), a playful, romantic story with just a touch of suspense. Beautiful academic Lauri Fields finds herself immediately at odds with devilishly enticing Adam Brady when he won't return some love letters written by her late grandfather. Undaunted, Lauri is willing to do whatever it takes to persuade this handsome charmer to give back what's rightfully hers. But Brady employs his own brand of seduction to teach Lauri a delightful lesson . . . What fun!

Readers love the provocative openings of Jan Mathews's romances, and in *Shady Lady* (#306), she's written another hot one. This time beautiful undercover police officer Catherine Coulton is posing as a prostitute, hoping to make a quick arrest, when aggressive Nick Samuels, also an undercover cop, comes on to her like gang busters! By blending madcap humor, gritty realism, and heart-melting romance, Jan stamps *Shady Lady* with her own distinctive style. She doesn't shy away from tough subjects—after all, her husband's a policeman—but she always touches the vulnerable core of her characters . . . and the heart of every romance reader.

It's been awhile since we've published a romance by Helen Carter, whose emotionally charged love stories have earned her wide recognition among readers. In *Tender Is the Night* (#307), hero Chris Carpenter is enthralled by heroine Toni Kendall's beauty, intelligence, and sense of fun. He's also drawn to her loving, zany family, something he's never had. But though he vows to make Toni his own, she seems determined to remain fancy free—and she may be destroying their best chance for happiness . . . Once again Helen Carter writes a complex and thoroughly satisfying story.

Here's a truly exceptional first romance by a terrific new talent—*For Love of Mike* (#308) by Courtney Ryan. Just when Gabby Cates should be flying the friendly skies to Hawaii with a brand-new husband, she's really stranded on a beach in a water-logged wedding dress with her overweight Siamese cat and tall, blond, slightly intoxicated Mike Hyatt. What's more, though she's escaped the net of marriage, she's lost her job and is about to be evicted from her home! Clearly, she needs help—and Mike's only too willing to oblige. *For Love of Mike* is wonderfully witty and delightfully unpredictable. Don't miss it!

What new romance includes a cheerleader named Olga who resembles a Nazi commandant, a couple of sidekicks called Killer and Tank, a heroine who's in big trouble because she's just paid seventeen million dollars for the *worst* football team in the league, and an original tough-guy quarterback who breaks every rule in the book? Why, the latest romance from Diana Morgan, of course! *Two in a Huddle* (#309) begins with Selena Derringer passing out in Trader O'Neill's arms. It ends with a wild football game. And what happens in the middle is loads of fun. Enjoy!

Until next month, happy reading,

Ellen Edwards

Ellen Edwards, Senior Editor
SECOND CHANCE AT LOVE
The Berkley Publishing Group
200 Madison Avenue
New York, NY 10016

P.S. Don't forget that our new SECOND CHANCE AT LOVE covers begin with the February books. Every bookseller and reviewer who has seen them loves them!

Second Chance at Love®

TWO
IN A HUDDLE

DIANA MORGAN

**A SECOND CHANCE AT LOVE
BOOK**

Second Chance at Love books are published by
The Berkley Publishing Group
200 Madison Avenue, New York, NY 10016

To Joan Marlow,
who can handle us

TWO
IN A HUDDLE

- *1* -

"FIVE SHOTS OF tequila, please."

The bartender looked a little stunned as Selena Derringer plunked down on a bar stool and began to savagely undo the tabs that fastened her brand-new winter coat.

"You heard me," she said dully. "Five shots, right up front, and five slices of lemon." Her voice was husky but tantalizingly feminine, and the meaning in her luminous brown eyes was clear. She intended to get completely and hopelessly drunk.

As she fumbled with the last of the tabs on her coat, she became suddenly aware that everybody in the place was staring at her. The after-work Wall Street crowd in their conservative pinstripes and London Fog raincoats apparently wasn't used to the spectacle of a well-dressed female drunk. Selena suspected that she was providing them with the best entertainment they had had all day.

Several pairs of eyes veered boldly in her direction, waiting to see what she would do next. Only the man sitting next to her placidly stirring the lemon twist in his drink seemed to remain uninterested in her antics.

Selena struggled impatiently with the stubborn tab. "Brrrr," she said, shivering, "it must be below zero out there." She continued addressing the bartender, who regarded her with a practiced poker face as if no one else in the bar were listening. "Honestly, I don't know how you New Yorkers can stand this rotten weather."

"You'd better get used to it, Selena."

She stopped wrestling with the tab and jerked around to stare at the man sitting next to her. How had he known her name? He was impeccably clad in a charcoal-gray three-piece suit, and his black hair was sprinkled with dashes of gray. Ivy League, she calculated automatically. An overgrown preppie who liked to provoke women in bars. Here in New York, she knew, strange men should be shunned at all costs. Keen, very blue eyes stared back at her, momentarily making her forget to give him the cold shoulder. He smiled suddenly, revealing perfect white teeth, and something in her memory stirred.

"I know you!" she cried, pointing a finger at him. "You were just upstairs, weren't you? I remember seeing you at the back of the room while the bids were being opened."

He nodded deferentially. "Unfortunately," he said

dryly, "my bid wasn't quite as high as yours." He reached over and easily snapped open the troublesome tab on her coat, letting it fall open. The movement was unexpectedly erotic somehow. He gazed boldly at her simple but elegant ivory knitted dress. It was straight-lined and sleek, but the rich, soft fabric did not fail to disclose her gentle curves. It contrasted dramatically with her short, stylishly cut black hair, which sparkled with crystal lights.

"Congratulations," he said, lifting his glass to her in a toast. "You and your brother Henry are now the proud owners of the Los Angeles Aces." He held up a hand to correct himself. "Or should I say the Brooklyn Aces? That is where Derringer Industries is relocating them, isn't it?"

Selena let out a defeated sigh, roundly confirming his guess. "Brooklyn," she muttered. "Of all places."

"It's a good choice," he disagreed candidly, sitting back to study her. Expensively and chicly dressed, she knew she stood out among the conservative gray flannels that populated the bar. "Brooklyn has the available stadium, for one thing," he elaborated. "And the town never got over the loss of the Dodgers . . . to Los Angeles," he finished pointedly. Selena didn't answer, and he continued in his infuriatingly conversational tone. "So, how does it feel to own the worst team in the National Football League?"

She was spared the necessity of a response by the arrival of five empty shot glasses, which the bartender lined up on the bar in front of her. He held the bottle of tequila up over the empty glasses, waiting for her to give him the go-ahead, and she nodded to him in an affirmative gesture.

"Fill 'em up," she said recklessly.

Each glass was filled to the very top, and five lemon slices were placed neatly next to each one. The bartender added a salt shaker, shook his head wearily, and strolled to the other end of the bar as if wanting to avoid the sight of a certain fiasco. Selena ignored him. She licked her index finger and sprinkled some salt on it, preparing to down her first shot.

"Better throw some of that salt over your shoulder for good luck," the stranger said. "You're going to need it. You're also going to need backers with a lot of capital. You may have bought a football team, but you don't have the cash necessary to make it work."

She stopped his needling with a quick, pointed shot from her dark eyes. "And how do you know that?" she demanded.

"I read your corporate prospectus," he explained rather smugly. "This purchase just cleaned you out."

"Don't be too sure of that," she said evenly. "After all, do you really think we'd jeopardize the family business?" She turned away, satisfied with her show of strength, but he was right, and she knew it. Her brother had staked all the capital they had into bidding for the Aces. Now Henry was thinking of selling off his own interest in Derringer Industries. That thought was so disheartening to Selena that it was easy for her to down the first shot of tequila. She bit into the lemon, closing her eyes for a second to savor the tart sensation after the sting of the liquor. Then she faced the blue-eyed stranger again, bolstered by a new piece of ammunition.

"My brother does have a few Aces up his sleeve— if you'll pardon the pun."

He picked up a lemon slice and smiled sardonically. "Pardon *my* pun, but you just bought a lemon with no fruit inside. The Aces need fresh new blood, and good players cost money. You don't even have a quarterback."

"A what?" she asked crossly.

"A quarterback. You know, the guy who throws the ball. Not having a quarterback in football is like playing baseball without a pitcher." He eyed her disdainfully, his opinion of her evidently dropping by the minute. "Do you mean to tell me you just spent seventeen million dollars on a team and you don't know anything about the game?"

That was enough to make her go another round of tequila. She drained the second shot, and another lemon rind took its place unceremoniously on top of the first.

"You may as well admit it," he prodded. "You're in big trouble."

The shot glass dropped onto the bar with a bang. Selena was tired of putting up defenses. She was tired of the whole thing. "Okay—so we're in trouble," she conceded with more bravado than she felt. "So what?" The tequila must have been having a fast effect on her, because she answered her own question before she could stop herself. "So, this might break us, that's all," she mumbled. She let out a long sigh and turned to face this confident man who seemed to know everything about her. His expression had changed from challenging to sympathetic, soothingly inviting her trust. "I love my brother," she said slowly as the tequila stole its way into her system, "but he had no business putting everything we have into a second-rate football team."

The stranger chuckled softly. "Then you should have stopped him."

Selena threw back her head and let out a short, humorless laugh. "Hardly. If you read our prospectus, then you also know that Henry is the major shareholder. He has the controlling interest, and he likes to control. Besides, no one could stop Henry from owning the only thing he ever wanted in his life. That man lives and breathes football. Do you know that he once lost out on a major sale because the client wanted to have a meeting during Monday night football?"

"But he still managed to increase Derringer Industries sales by thirty percent in the past two years," the man observed smoothly, disconcerting her with his knowledge about her company. "Sent your stocks shooting sky-high. Not bad for a Sunday afternoon armchair quarterback."

Selena frowned, not because he was right again, but because he had just missed a crucial and annoyingly obvious point. "Did it ever occur to you that I may have had something to do with that?" she asked sharply. "After all, I am vice-president of the company."

"Oh, I haven't forgotten that," he said airily. "Not at all. I'm beginning to wish I could."

"Why?" she asked sharply.

"Because it's so obviously wrong for you." His eyes swept candidly over her lithe form, sending a swift, breathless message of sexuality that stunned her.

Selena opened her mouth to berate him, fighting the unbidden tide of physical response that was coursing treacherously through her body. But he cut her off dismissively. "Spare me, Selena. I can see what you're thinking. I'm sure you're a perfectly respectable vice-president. Profit and loss, marketing, PR—all of that. But I don't think a fascinating woman like you could have much interest in paper boxes." His incredibly blue eyes tingled with amusement. "I know your father built the company up from nothing and I respect that. But what does it leave for you? Is manufacturing paper boxes your lifelong dream? Somehow I doubt that. It just doesn't seem a fitting vocation for the only woman ever to have made the rowing team at UCLA. As well as," he continued, evidently unabashed in the face of her mounting unease at his array of knowledge, "the winner of the jewelry design contest in art school."

Selena stared at him, astonished. "I only went to art school for a year," she said uncomfortably. "Then I transferred to business. How did you know that, anyway?"

"I did my homework," he answered briefly. His hands reached out and fingered the unusual pendant that hung from a slender chain around her neck. It was a tiny jeweled carving of a dolphin jumping playfully from stylized waves. "You're very good," he commented, taking it for granted that she had made the carving herself. "I hope you haven't stopped designing jewelry."

"We all have to grow up and accept adult responsibilities sometime," Selena countered. "I have no time for such frivolities anymore, especially now that the company is moving. This transfer will take up all my time."

"If creative achievement is your idea of frivolity, then you really do have a problem," he remarked.

Selena was getting tired of his jibes. "For the moment," she said testily, determined to close the subject, "all this vice-president has on her mind is how to keep her business from sinking."

He lifted his glass and saluted her. "Welcome to New York City, Madame Vice-President," he said sounding a little disappointed in her. "If you think the winters are cold, wait until you feel the humidity and heat of our infernal summers." With the air of a conqueror, he turned back to the bar and nursed his drink.

Selena stared at him, aghast. "I suppose you think you know all about it," she fumed, preparing to begin a final and utterly scathing tirade against him. "If you knew anything about business, you'd know that it doesn't really matter what the product is. Business skills are always the same." She frowned darkly, cursing the tequila. It was making it very hard for her to concentrate. "It just so happens that I love my work," she continued self-righteously. "And Derringer Industries has expanded from simply making paper boxes."

"Hurray," he said mockingly. "I understand you made a big move last year into corrugated cardboard. Exciting."

"What's wrong with it?" she cried. "And what's the matter with *you?* Did you follow me here just to insult me because you're a sore loser?"

He looked genuinely surprised. "Of course not," he said loftily. "Besides, I didn't follow you. I was here first, remember?" He paused to sip his drink. "It's just that I have a terrible weakness for beautiful women with sad eyes."

"My eyes are not sad," Selena said savagely, repeating each word with distinct emphasis. "I am a very happy person."

"Then what are you doing in this bar with five shots of tequila?" he asked flatly. His arm reached toward her and she shrank back. "Look at you," he chided, his long fingers closing around her delicate forearm. "You're afraid of me. I'm sorry, Selena." His tone was so warm and soothing that she almost trembled under his touch. "I can see such hidden passion in you, just waiting to be brought out."

"Is that so?" she retorted. "And I suppose you're the proper person to do it. How very lucky for me. I get a football team and a savior, all in one miserable day."

"I'm talking about all kinds of passion," he insisted, his fingers beginning a gentle massage that sent darts of fire into her blood. "Passion for your work is just as important as other kinds. Paper boxes just don't express you. And I really don't think football does either."

"I have absolutely no desire to own a football team," she muttered helplessly, the tequila and his persistent touch putting reckless words into her mouth. "And in Brooklyn!" She shook her head with tipsy remorse. "Just where the hell is Brooklyn, anyway?"

Without looking up, the man pointed past her nose with his free hand. The other hand was still resting intimately on her arm. "Thataway," he said. "Right over the Brooklyn Bridge. Or you can take the Brooklyn Battery Tunnel or the Williamsburg Bridge. A lot of people simply walk. I understand that's a rarity in your hometown of Los Angeles. An acute lack of sidewalks, or something like that."

His hand left her arm abruptly, and he eyed her critically, his steely blue eyes roving candidly over her elegant but defeated form. He had an air of awesome control that should have been intimidating. Instead, it was keenly attractive. Through the haze of heady intoxication that was mercifully obscuring her judgment, Selena had a flash of insight that would have remained dormant if she had stayed sober. She caught her breath slightly as she recognized the sweet, sinking sensation. How I would love to be in his arms, she thought brazenly. He's so very sexy. Almost immediately, she shook herself back to awareness. The man was clearly too intelligent to toy with. She would have to be very, very careful with him. Without even trying, he might trip her up and make her regret something she said or did. She eyed him with new wariness, trying valiantly to look tough, yet she had a vague idea that her attempt was ridiculous; her words were already beginning to slur and the determined expression on her glazed face felt more comical than serious.

He witnessed this flutter of varying emotions on her face with measured consideration.

But Selena shook her head stubbornly, refusing to concede anything at all to this compelling man who was affecting her in a most disturbing way. "You're obviously as upset about not getting the Aces as I am about buying them," she said boldly, deliberately starting a new confrontation.

"That's an understatement." He swallowed the last of his drink and motioned to the bartender for another one. It was supplied quickly, and he took a long sip before facing her again.

Selena was frowning, trying to figure out his motives. "But—but if the Aces are as bad as all that, why did you want them so much?" she blurted out.

For the first time, she seemed to have found a chink in his armor. "It's just a crazy fantasy," he said abruptly. "I guess I'm a little too old for that sort of dreaming."

"What sort of dreaming is that?" she pried. She stared baldly at him, her doubts filtering suddenly through her deceptively pleasant tequila haze. "Just who are you, anyway?" she demanded.

He was totally unintimidated by her sharp tone, and he took his time before answering. "I'm a man," he said somberly, "who has just lost out on a very rare opportunity." His eyes hammered into her to see if she understood. "A second chance," he stated. "A second chance." He lifted his glass bitterly and drained it until nothing was left but the lime twist and the ice cubes that clinked decisively as he slapped the glass back on the bar.

"Another one," he said to the bartender.

There was a pause while Selena digested his enigmatic disclosures. He seemed to be a man of conviction, but she still had no idea what he was talking about. "A second chance?" she repeated slowly. "At what?" She considered his commanding air, and took a wild guess. "Are you a football coach?"

He laughed shortly, as if at some private joke. "Actually, I do coach a Little League team in Brooklyn. "But, no, coaching isn't my line of work. What I really want to do is—" He stopped to look sternly at her face, and decided against going further.

"Go on," she coaxed. "You were saying? What you really want to do is—"

The bartender placed his drink down and the stranger

immediately lifted it up and swallowed half of it in one gulp.

Selena watched him admiringly and then joined him. "To dashed dreams and losing teams," she toasted with drunken gallantry. Without missing a beat, she quickly downed the third shot of tequila, ignoring the disapproving look on her companion's face. This shot hit home, and she realized that she was swaying slightly on the stool. When she gazed up at him, he was busy stirring his drink.

"You know something?" she said, her speech slurring. "If you love football so much, perhaps I can offer you a job."

"What?" He dropped the swizzle stick abruptly and whipped around to face her.

"After all," she reminded him. "That team is half mine. And if I want to hire someone," she said firmly, giving him a resounding slap on the back, "then I'll hire someone." The room was beginning to spin, but she ignored it, concentrating on making her point. "Of course," she added slyly, "you don't really need a job, do you? If you can afford to buy the Aces, you don't need any money."

One black eyebrow arched menacingly as his eyes bored into her. "I assure you," he said in adament tones that made her sit up and blink, "money has nothing to do with it."

She absorbed this for a moment, and then affected a shrug. "So then, what do you say? Do you want that second chance?"

"What?"

"A job," she said pointedly. "I'm offering you a job." She was no longer sure her words were coming out as she intended them to, especially when he burst out laughing. She stared at him with drunken candor, wondering what she had said to amuse him, and he gave her an incredulous grin in return.

"You're serious about this, aren't you?" he asked.

Selena nodded gleefully.

"Can I have my choice of jobs?" he continued playfully.

"Of course," she said expansively, fancying that she sounded serious and professional. "Just as long as you're qualified."

"Sounds fair," he said with a straight face.

She was now very drunk, she realized. "You can apply for any position except vice-president," she informed him judiciously. "That's my job. My brother is the president. You probably can't have his job, either, but if you really want it, I'll see what I can do." Her voice had taken on a conspiratorial tone, as if she were doing him a great favor.

He laughed delightedly and took a sip of his drink.

"What's so funny?" she demanded.

"Nothing—anymore," he said, frowning a moment as he considered her rash offer. "You just gave me that second chance." He saluted her and downed the rest of his drink. His face was now unmistakably happy, but even in her drunken state Selena could see the wheels in his head turning with some new calculation.

"Bartender," he called out authoritatively, "drinks for the house are on me!"

A hum of approval and appreciation went through the bar as people heard him, and the bartender turned to acknowledge him with a nod.

"To second chances," Selena toasted wildly, clinking her glass against his. The fourth shot of tequila went through her like lightning, and her head left her body and floated somewhere above her shoulders.

"Oooh," she purred. "That last one was a killer." She tried to focus on the stranger, but his powerful body seemed to split into two halves. The two parts joined together for one maddening moment and then split apart again, hovering resolutely next to the bar. "How do you manage to hold your liquor?" she asked, noting his control. "You've had just as many drinks as I have."

He said nothing as a sardonic grin flashed across his face, and Selena reached out and took the glass from his hand. Holding it directly under her nose, she gave him a puzzled look and took a tentative sip.

"It tastes like club soda," she announced.

"It *is* club soda," he answered. "I don't drink when I'm in training."

She had trouble digesting that remark as her head became numb and her eyes glazed over. "In training?" she repeated. "In training for what?"

"Why, for my job interview—of course. Unless you're reneging on your offer already?"

"Of course not," Selena said staunchly. She reached out to assure him that all was well, but she lost her balance and slipped off the stool. Her arms flailed out to reach for the bar, but fortunately his arm was there to stop her. With one decisive motion, he caught her before she fell, and he placed her back on the stool as if she were a rag doll.

"Careful there," he admonished.

"I guess I'm a little unsteady. Whoops!" Again she

almost keeled over, but at the last minute she grabbed his arm and boosted herself up. The arm remained there for a few seconds like an object in a dream, and she examined it with interest. To her consternation, it was as solid as an iron pole.

"My God," she said, punching it lightly. "It's as hard as a rock." She continued to push drunkenly at the man's arm, but it didn't budge. Not even when she used both hands and put all her weight into it, was she able to move the arm an inch. "What are you?" she asked. "The Bionic Man? This arm feels like a steel rod."

"That's my throwing arm," he explained briefly, but there was a challenge in his voice that made her look up. "Now about that tryout," he continued, as if she knew exactly what he meant.

"Tryout?" she repeated dizzily.

"Yes, for the job you promised me. Or are you too drunk to recall our recent conversation?"

She was very mixed up, but she tried valiantly to answer him intelligently. "Just exactly what position are you interested in applying for?"

He smiled confidently. "Why, quarterback, of course."

Selena did a comical double take. "You've got to be putting me on."

"I'm interested in playing football," he returned steadily. "And I assure you, this is no joke."

"Playing!" She didn't want to be rude, but he had to be kidding. He couldn't be a day under thirty-three—much too old to start butting heads with beefy kids in their prime. That was the main problem with the Aces. Most of the players were over the hill, and according to Henry, players over thirty were old men. She looked him over once more. Even in her drunken state, she could see that he had kept himself in excellent shape, but to actually play professional ball—that was nothing short of madness! "May I ask you a blunt question?" she blurted out.

"I'm thirty-five," he replied at once, throwing her a knowing look. "Does that answer your question?"

"And you want to try out for this team?"

He nodded with a gleeful determination that plainly told her he meant it.

"How long do you think you can last?" she asked flatly. "The rest of the team will slaughter you."

He merely shrugged, his clear eyes twinkling.

"You really mean this," she observed.

He nodded seriously, and Selena couldn't control the smirk on her face. Before she could help it, she found herself laughing uncontrollably.

"Am I that amusing?" he asked. His china-blue eyes seemed to burn through her, and for one brief moment she was mesmerized by their intensity.

"Amusing?" she asked, faltering. "Uh—no. Not at all. In fact, I've got a wonderful idea. Why don't you just truck on down to the stadium when they start their tryouts, or whatever they're called, and I'll give you a personal interview."

"That's all I'm asking."

She stared at him in disbelief until, finally, unable to control herself, she started laughing again. But her laughter was stopped quickly by the look on his face. Leaning on the bar for support, she began shaking her head as if their entire conversation had been a dream. He hadn't moved the whole time and she could feel

his eyes boring into her. Well, she thought, she had
somehow promised to give him that second chance
he had been talking about. She knew she wouldn't
back out now, even if she later regretted her impulse.
He had just lost the chance to own the team she didn't
want; the least she could do was give him an opportunity to try out for quarterback.

But there was more than just that. She looked up
at him groggily, searching his stern, angular face for
a clue. What kind of a man, she wondered, would be
willing to spend millions of dollars to purchase an
entire football team just so that he could play on it?
The forceful drive inside him was startingly clear to
her. It fascinated her and attracted her at the same
time, but some instinct that was born of femininity
rather than business sense told her to conceal it.

"So, Mr. Quarterback," Selena said unevenly,
averting her eyes from his powerful gaze. "Do you
have a name?"

He hesitated a second, seeming reluctant to tell
her. "Trader," he answered finally, retreating behind
his glass.

"Trader," she repeated dreamily. "Trader what?"

"Just Trader. It's a nickname."

She lifted her drink in front of his nose and patted
his shoulder approvingly. "Here's to you, Mr. Trader
the Elderly Quarterback. May your second chance be
a success."

"And to you, Selena Derringer," he added gallantly. "May you follow your star, wherever it may
lead you."

Down went the drink, hitting her stomach like a
bomb. For one dizzying second, she thought she saw

Trader's arm going back to throw her a long pass. He was dressed in a football jersey and she was running to catch the football. But somehow she missed and came crashing into his strong arms. Her mind began to fade in and out, and the last thing she remembered clearly was nestling against the shelter of his powerful chest, softly murmuring, "Touchdown, Trader. Touchdown . . ."

- 2 -

FOUR MONTHS LATER, Selena watched New York City welcome its new football team with open arms. The day before summer practice was to start, the Aces arrived at Kennedy Airport from L. A. and were treated to a ticker-tape parade down Flatbush Avenue in the heart of Brooklyn. Sleek open cars decorated with streamers and paper flowers snaked their way through the borough, and throngs of new fans lined the streets with banners and flags of their own. The gaudy pizza parlors, the darkened Irish bars, the huge discount furniture stores, and the little mom-and-pop candy stores that had been there for a quarter of a century all displayed hand-painted signs that extolled the Aces and urged them on to victory in the fall. Selena sat with her brother in the lead car, waving to the fans and smiling at the television cameras. Henry was in his element, she noted, reveling in the attention and excitement. But Selena had other things on her mind.

From the moment he had bought the team, Henry had busily spent all his time—and unhappily, all of his assets as well—on acquiring new players, forcing Selena to devote all of *her* time to working at the new corporate headquarters six blocks from the stadium.

It had been a complicated move for her, and she was still adjusting. New York had a pace and a personality that was light years away from Los Angeles. There were times when she thought it would have been simpler to move to another country.

She had few friends, although she was self-sufficient enough not to mind this for a while, at least. There were times, late at night mostly, alone in her bed, when she would summon the memory of two vivid blue eyes that had awakened her deepest responses. She wondered idly who the man really was, and whether she would ever see him again. He hadn't appeared in the last four months, and it seemed logical that he never would. He had only been taunting her, playing with her growing state of intoxication. She was mildly surprised that this stranger had so easily replaced thoughts of Todd, her former fiancé, with whom she had broken up several months before. She had easily outdistanced Todd a long time ago, but it had taken her a while to see it. Now she saw that any lingering memories of Todd had been mere remnants. He no longer held any place in her heart.

But these thoughts only intruded when she let them, which wasn't often. There was no time for dreaming.

Her personal state of mind was a minor subject compared to the havoc her brother had wreaked on the family business.

In no time at all, Henry had jeopardized Derringer Industries for the sake of the Aces, and it was almost inevitable that if left to his own devices, he would bankrupt the company. After a moment of panic, Selena had rolled up her sleeves and had quickly discovered a special knack that had been dormant for years, just waiting for the opportunity to surface in the face of an emergency. Henry was only too glad for the help, unofficially handing over the reins of the presidency to her so that he could devote all his time to the team. In the span of a few short months, Selena had managed to keep the company above water. But it had become a hopeless game of recouping losses. Every time she turned a profit, Henry would take the money and buy a new star player.

His most recent purchase was now costing them a million dollars, and to make matters worse, the company had just lost a vital government contract. It was time for Selena to put her foot down.

Arriving two hours early on the first day of practice, she found the stadium a cold, ghostly place. Although it was well over seventy degrees, the June sun could not heat the skeleton of girders and harsh gray bricks that made up the inner corridor. Deliberately shutting out the memory of California sunshine, Selena listened to the dull echo of her footsteps as she walked through the tunnel that led onto the open playing field. She was dressed in a crisp white suit with a single strand of pearls and a dashing navy fedora, but her face was set with a tension that had become second nature to her since she had assumed the executive spot. As she approached the end of the tunnel, she pulled the tip of her hat over her eyes in order to shadow the sunlight. When her eyes finally adjusted, she blinked uncertainly at the strange sight that greeted her on the field.

Sitting in the middle of the fifty-yard line was the mysterious man she had met in the bar on that awful day when Henry had bought the Aces. She recognized him almost instantly. There was something about the powerful, uncompromising set of his shoulders and the way he stared so intently at the goalpost that reminded her of the crazy conversation they had had— and of the reckless promise she had made him. She had wondered guiltily about that, but since he had never materialized, she had never had to come up with an answer.

He didn't hear as she approached, and she stared down at him curiously. He seemed to be meditating, or concentrating intently on some inner vision. He looked quite comfortable and relaxed, wearing a faded blue and gold football jersey, and she had the uneasy feeling that if she didn't talk to him, he might just sit there all day, as peaceful as Ferdinand the Bull.

"Hey!" she called from the bleachers. "Long time no see. How's it going?"

He turned slowly and looked her over, his shrewd eyes raking over her trim figure with uncanny frankness.

"New York hasn't changed you," he pronounced after a merciless inspection. "But something else has. You're a lot different from the last time I saw you."

He was different, too, but she didn't say so. There

was now an invisible barrier between them, one that kept the electric attraction they felt for each other temporarily at bay. He was here for a reason, and everything else would come second to that. She gazed at his uniform with trepidation, knowing all too well why he was here. "You're serious about trying out for the team, aren't you?" she asked directly.

He looked at the goalpost, not at her. "I've never been more serious."

"Well," she faltered, "I did say I'd give you an interview."

"Yes, you did," he agreed promptly. "A personal one."

Selena was annoyed suddenly. She would have to live up to her promise, but she knew it was a waste of time. This man who called himself Trader was obviously too old to play pro ball with a bunch of beefy kids in their prime. Did he think she didn't know that? "All right," she said in a clipped tone. "Let's get going. You want a tryout? You've got it. Right now."

He didn't react, and Selena marched over to the benches where a bag full of footballs lay on the ground. She dumped them all out, letting them bounce crazily at her feet, and after a moment of deliberation, she chose one.

"Here we go," she said, palming the ball in her hand. "A brand-new one." Without warning, she tossed it playfully toward Trader, but her aim was off, and it arced high over his head. She thought he would let it hit the ground and then scoop it up, but she was totally unprepared for the precision of his reflexes. In that split-second, he jumped from a sitting position at least three feet into the air. His feet kicked up, bending behind him to push him even higher, and his hands wrapped easily around the ball, snapping it into the pit of his flat stomach. He came down lightly, landing with the same serious look on his face.

"Not bad." Selena tried to feign coolness. "Not bad at all—for an old man."

"Go out for a button hook," he ordered her. "I'll hit you at the forty."

"What?" she gaped. "What's that?"

"Go on," he repeated. "Run."

She looked down at her high heels and the trim lines of her white business suit. She was dressed for a business meeting, not for a quickie romp on the field. Her hand touched the brim of her navy fedora with its broad white band. "Couldn't we just make it a simple catch?" she asked dryly. It wasn't just her suit that was making her edgy. It was the uncanny ability of this man to one-up everything she did.

He shook his head, and with a devil-may-care shrug, Selena found herself kicking off her shoes and removing her suit jacket. When she glanced up, she saw that he was watching her appreciatively, and her own eyes narrowed. If he was baiting her, she intended to give him a run for his money.

"All set," she said energetically. She ran in place a few times as if to limber up, but he was not amused.

"The hat," he noted impatiently, using the football as a pointer. "Take it off."

She smiled politely, letting him know that she would humor him only so far, but he remained quite determined. "Look," she said, trying a more reasonable tone. "Couldn't we just throw a few and—"

"Take it off," he ordered; and then, as if to impress upon her his intentions, he aimed the football directly at her. She realized with no small irritation that he was preparing to knock the hat off her head.

"You wouldn't dare," she challenged, her dark eyes astonished.

"Want to bet?" He wound back his throwing arm, limbering up as his eyes assessed the distance from the ball to her hat.

The crazy thing was, she was starting to believe he could actually do it. "Look, William Tell," she said firmly, "if you think you can knock this hat from my head at twenty yards—"

She stared at the football that was aimed menacingly at her, and decided that maybe he had a point. She was not about to stand there like a performing seal in a circus, waiting for him to make a fool of her. "Okay, okay!" she conceded, holding her hands in front of her face in case he decided to actually attempt the feat. "You win—for now." Off came the hat, and Selena walked bravely onto the field, prepared to take him on. "I'm ready when you are."

"Fine," he said calmly. "Now, without looking back at me, I want you to run all the way down to the twenty-yard line and then quickly turn around."

"Why?" she asked darkly.

He sighed impatiently. "You'll find a football in your stomach. Try to hold on to it."

She gave him a baleful look, and reviewed his instructions aloud. "Run to the twenty, don't look back, then turn around. Sounds easy enough," she allowed. *Okay, wise guy,* she added silently, *let's see your stuff.* Eyeing his powerful stance, she took a deep breath and faced him boldly.

He said nothing, merely grinning at her with a wicked "you'll-see" glint in his eyes, and she knew she was in for it. With new determination, she began the run, carefully noting the white yard markings.

"Keep going," he called out from behind her. "Lift those legs higher!"

What am I, a dancer? she thought, her temper rising again. Who is this guy to be giving me orders? He sounds as if *he* owns the team.

"Faster, and don't look back!" Trader ordered.

Selena clamped her teeth together and kept running. This had better be good, she thought. But she wasn't going to slow down and give him a chance to back out.

"That's it!" he called. "Good."

His voice jolted her into an even faster pace, and she began to feel distinctly foolish. Why was she racing down the length of a stadium in her stockinged feet, simply because some cocky newcomer with devilish eyes had ordered her to? As she reached the twenty-yard line, she heard his voice again, piercing her rebellious thoughts.

"Now!" he ordered, *"Turn!"*

She whipped around on instinct, and to her utter surprise, found a football impaled in her stomach.

"Oof!" was the only sound she made as the force of the impact threw her to the ground. She rolled over, clutching blindly at the ball in her middle, not even sure if the gasp that followed came from her.

"Good catch!" Trader called out heartily, as if he were the coach. "Let's try that again, only this time I want you to double back and—" He stopped talking when it became apparent that she wasn't getting up.

"What hit me?" she asked as a pair of very strong arms lifted her to a sitting position.

"You'll be all right in a second," he assured her. "You just got the wind knocked out of you." He began expertly massaging her stomach, the warmth of his hands stealing through the cool fabric of her suit. "Better?" he asked, continuing the soothing strokes.

She didn't answer, mostly because she couldn't, but also because he was definitely affecting her in a way that brought the scene of their first meeting back to her in a rush. His face was very close to hers, and she observed breathlessly that it was oddly off-balance, the features strong but asymmetrical. It was a stubborn face, and a paradoxical one. She couldn't understand how it managed to be so attractive despite its lack of conventional beauty. And he looked quite gentle for a man who had just tried to put a hole in her stomach.

"I'm impressed, Derringer." He said her last name as if she were a fellow teammate. She almost expected him to slap her roughly on the back, and she frowned at the camaraderie. She didn't want him to treat her as one of the guys. She was, after all, part owner of this team.

Trader, however, was enthusiastic. "You may not know football," he said, "but you're not afraid to try your hand at it, are you?" He smiled and shook his head. "If you handle your father's company the way you just handled that football, there may be hope for you yet."

"And what is that supposed to mean?" she asked, finally regaining her breath. His arm was still around her, and neither one of them made any attempt to remove it.

"Let's just say that you didn't drop the ball." He

stood up, and she squinted at his figure as it was silhouetted against the strong sunlight.

"Who *are* you?" she asked suddenly, point-blank.

"I'm your new quarterback."

"And how do you know I'll hire you?"

"The same way I know you won't let Derringer Industries go without a fight. Paper boxes may not be your true calling, but I hear you've been giving it an A-1 effort."

"Thank you," she said coolly. He extended his hand to help her up, but instead of taking it, she pushed it aside and stood up on her own.

As she brushed herself off, Trader grinned appreciatively, looking her up and down. "Not bad, Derringer," he commented judiciously. "Not bad at all." She looked up quickly. Was he still talking about her talents?

"That's Ms. Derringer," she said evenly.

He backed off for a moment and shook his head. "Selena," he said quietly. He spoke her name with a respect that startled her, and she realized that he wasn't baiting her.

"Listen, William Tell," she said, swallowing hard. "You're a good shot with the football, but I'm not the one to talk to. Hang around for another hour until the coach shows up. If he says you're good, and if my brother, Henry, approves—" She let the sentence hang there, and Trader gave her a melting smile.

"That's all I'm asking."

There was a long silence, during which they exchanged a look that made everything else seem irrelevant. It crept slowly into her blood, making her fingertips tingle with unexpected anticipation, and for one crazy moment she pictured him with a bow and arrow trying to shoot an apple from her head. He smiled enigmatically, and there was no way to tell what was going on behind those striking blue eyes. Selena only hoped he couldn't read *her* thoughts.

Without another word, she went over to the sidelines to retrieve her jacket and shoes. The large navy hat was still on the ground, and she brushed it off before clapping it back on her head.

"See you later, William Tell," she said without turning around. She headed over to the bleachers, knowing perfectly well that those laser eyes of his were still boring into her. Some unnamed strategy prevented her from looking back, no matter how curious she was. It was fortunate she didn't, for the next instant she was given the biggest surprise of her life.

From out of nowhere, the football came smashing against the steps ten feet in front of her, knocking her hat neatly off her head in the process. It made her jump in alarm, which was emphasized by the stunning impact of his precision. She picked her hat up slowly, peculiarly out of breath and completely aghast at what he had done. When she finally managed to look back at him, her face registering her awe, she saw that he had resumed his original position on the fifty-yard line, as if he had never budged.

The stadium office was located sixty feet above the fifty-yard line, halfway between the box seats and top row bleachers. It had a huge picture window that could be rolled back for a perfect view of the game, and luxurious sofas as well as a bar and kitchenette. The large oak desk against the back wall had a com-

fortably upholstered swivel chair in which Selena's
brother, Henry, usually sat. From this throne, he could
easily communicate with his coaches on the field
through myriad futuristic technical devices that ranged
from a walkie-talkie to a loudspeaker that was ten
decibels higher than the announcer's.

After fixing herself an Alka-seltzer, Selena plopped
herself down at the desk and gazed out over the field.
She could see the lone figure in his jersey still sitting
peacefully, exactly as she had left him.

Shrugging, she downed the seltzer. If Trader had
ever played before, she reasoned, Henry would probably know of him.

But Henry drew a blank as well. When he finally
showed up—an hour later and sporting his usual uniform of a tailored suit with crew socks and sneakers—
he merely scratched his head and shrugged.

"Never saw him before, but that's a University of
Michigan jersey he's got on," he drawled. "And anyone who used to play for the Wolverines can't be all
bad, right?" He winked, but Selena wasn't ready to
humor him. Pushing away from the desk, she scolded
her brother for his tardiness.

"Where have you been all this time? You were
supposed to meet me here an hour ago."

Henry completely ignored the question. "You know
something crazy?" he asked, glancing again at the
man on the field. "I think I *have* seen him before."
He reached around the desk and pulled out a pair of
binoculars. "The face looks familiar," he said as he
focused the lens, "but I can't place the year or the
position."

"Try quarterback," Selena said curiously.

Henry gave her a sharp glance before resuming his spying. "Maybe... He's certainly got the right build for it, doesn't he?"

"I don't know." Selena sighed. She was forced to rely on Henry for that kind of information, despite her growing uneasiness about her brother's lack of objectivity. He had made adequate decisions about Derringer Industries until they had acquired the Aces. Now, he was so gung-ho about the team that she feared he would do something really foolish out of his innocent enthusiasm.

Henry was a large, gangly, amiable fellow, two years Selena's senior, but to her mind he was still just an overgrown boy—much like the players he was so avidly hiring. She knew that as far as business went, she had no right to feel superior to him. After all, they had jointly agreed to take responsibility for the company after their father's death, and neither of them had much experience. But it was hard not to be impatient with Henry. Selena repressed a sigh and looked at him. He was still studying the newcomer with a shrewd expression, his suit hanging loosely on his lanky frame despite its careful tailoring. "So," she asked, "who is he?"

Henry shrugged again and put down the binoculars. "Your guess is as good as mine. Maybe he's looking for a job as a coach."

Selena chuckled. "Would you believe me if I told you that he's here to try out?"

"What?" Henry sputtered. "Don't be ridiculous. The guy must be at least thirty." At twenty-nine, Henry still thought that anyone over thirty belonged to another generation.

"Thirty-five," Selena corrected as she looked down at the field. "And his nickname is Trader. That's all I can tell you."

"Trader . . . Trader," Henry mused, searching his memory. "No, I still can't place him. I can't remember anyone by that name."

The Aces were starting to trickle out onto the field in their gray practice jerseys, making the alien blue and gold stand out even more. Henry lifted the walkie-talkie from his desk and clicked on the transmitter. "Say, Eli? Eli, can you hear me?"

Down on the field, a stocky man in a navy blue athletic jacket adjusted the headphones over his ears and waved up at the office window.

"Loud and clear," came the voice over the box.

"See what that guy wants, would you?" Henry asked.

Eli waved and signed out, and Selena watched him walk over to Trader.

"So what is it that was so important you had to get me down here at eight in the morning?" Henry asked. He was still gazing at the players when Selena slapped a copy of the *Daily News* on his desk. Henry couldn't avoid cringing when he saw it, but he quickly recovered. "I've already seen that," he said, embarrassed. "It's not such a big deal." He decided to try going on the offensive. "Do you always get up so early? It must have been seven o'clock when you called."

"Six," Selena corrected, striking the newspaper with her hand. Holding it up in front of his face, she read the headline on one of the columns aloud. "'Henry Derringer Trades Stocks for a Tank.'" There was a picture of her brother standing next to a huge man holding a football helmet, both of them grinning wickedly at the camera like two schoolboys caught in a prank.

"According to the article," Selena said, stabbing the picture with her finger, "you paid a million dollars for this Neanderthal. Is that true?"

"Uh—not quite. Actually it was 1.2 million—but Tank Larson is worth his weight in gold," Henry added self-righteously.

Selena could hardly contain herself. "Do you realize that ever since you began this football adventure, our stock has tumbled to a record low of under five dollars a share? We're flirting with bankruptcy!"

Henry turned back to gaze down at the field where all the players were warming up. Trader was now talking with the coach, who was shaking his head stubbornly in response.

"Darn it," Henry said. "I've seen him before. I just can't remember where."

"Henry!" Selena raised her voice. "Are you listening to me? I am talking bankruptcy—as in *broke*."

Her brother ambled over and put his hand on her shoulder. "I know football, Selena," he explained stubbornly. "It's what I know best. Just trust me, will you?"

Selena looked back at him, hope mingled with fear. She wanted to believe him, but she didn't know at what point her faith in her brother became a sheer indulgence of his fantasy. Henry's maneuvers had played havoc with the stocks, and he had been so driven to build his dream team that he had staked every ounce of capital they had on it. Selena knew

they were stuck with the Aces. The only question was
how long they could hold on.

"Tell me, Henry," she said quietly, "just how good
is this team going to be? You do know your football,
I'll grant you that."

Henry looked at her earnestly. "It's shaping up,
Selena, honest." He hesitated. "There's only one problem." His attention was diverted by the sight of Trader
in his blue and gold jersey, throwing ball after ball
unerringly through the middle of a rubber tire that was
swinging back and forth from a pole. "Consistent,"
he muttered to himself. "Very consistent."

"Henry?" Selena said impatiently. "Never mind him.
What about the problem?" But her eyes betrayed her
and followed her brother's gaze. Trader was still
throwing balls like flying arrows, and his body in
motion was electric with agility and accuracy.

Henry turned to acknowledge her. "We need a first-
rate quarterback," he explained flatly, gesturing directly at the performance going on below them. He
paused, hypnotized by Trader's precision.

The intercom crackled on again. "Say, Henry?"

"Did you find out who that guy is, Eli?" Henry
said into the machine.

"Yeah. He wants to try out for the quarterback
spot."

"He's not bad," Henry said abruptly. "But he's a
little late getting started—like about ten years. We
can't waste our time trying out every amateur who
marches into the stadium."

"He's no amateur!" Selena surprised herself by defending Trader too hotly, and she bit her lip in confusion.

Henry threw her a quizzical glance. After all, Selena had never before been so excited about anything that had to do with the team.

"Why not try him out?" she suggested. "After all," she couldn't resist adding, "you're practically out of money, and quarterbacks don't come cheap."

There was a moment of silence as her brother weighed her words with some trepidation. "Okay, Eli, give him a shot," he decided. "Choose up two teams and have this guy play quarterback. I want to see him in action. But I want him put through the grinder— no holds barred. If he can pass muster, we'll let him stay on for a few weeks and see how he does." Henry was in command now, his eyes narrowing as he bit his lip. Selena did not even realize that she was smiling triumphantly. "And, Eli," Henry continued.

"Yeah?"

Henry looked at his sister curiously, as if wondering why she looked so happy. "Give him hell. If he's not going to cut it, we may as well find out now. I don't want to take him because he has a great throwing arm and then learn in midseason that he doesn't have the stamina to last through a game."

Selena was sobered by her brother's choice of words, but Henry did know his football. For once, she wasn't going to interfere. Trusting her brother's judgment, she sat nervously on the sofa for the next half hour and witnessed a veritable trial by fire.

Even to her inexperienced eyes, Trader was superb. Football had always seemed a maddeningly he-man game to her. A bunch of guys wearing padding and helmets that made them look like Martians would line up against each other on the field. One guy would get the ball, and he would try to break through the gorillas across from him. But he usually didn't get far. In seconds, a heap of players would pile on top of him, and then the whole thing would begin again. But today, watching Trader's powerful grace, Selena found that the game began to make sense to her. As the quarterback, he was the ringleader, the one who initiated all the moves. Under his deft control, his team inched their way across the field, gaining ground with every play.

"Not bad," Henry temporized after watching Trader's performance. "But Eli's being too easy on him. Let's see what our friend here can do in an emergency." He picked up the microphone, and to Selena's horror gave the ultimate command. "Okay, Eli," Henry said coldly, "kill him."

Selena gulped as she watched Eli acknowledge the command with a thumbs-up salute. "What's that supposed to mean?" she asked nervously.

But Henry merely gave her an evil smile and gestured down at the field. Trader had the ball and was moving back rapidly with his arm in the air, obviously ready to throw it. Abruptly, two opposing team members, both charging like elephants, broke through the line and came rushing at Trader. Selena cringed, anticipating the momentary impact, but it never came. At the last second, Trader cradled the football in his arms and evaded the two behemoths with lightning agility. Two more tackles came at him, but he darted around them like a rocket and headed down the field. Suddenly, there was nothing between Trader and the goalposts but open air.

"Go for it!" Henry yelled excitedly. "Run!"

As if Trader had actually heard Henry's words, he bolted straight ahead, sprinting freely for the goalpost. Two more players tried to run after him, but they never caught up with him as he crossed over into the end zone.

"Touchdown!" Selena cried, throwing her arms up over her head. She couldn't believe how exhilarated she felt, but she no longer cared that she was acting out of character. "Well, what do you say to that, tough guy?" she asked her brother triumphantly.

Henry couldn't hide the excitement on his face, but he was careful to remain conservative in his judgment. "Not bad," he quipped. "For an old man." He picked up the mike once more. "Okay, Eli, that's enough. We don't want to give the guy a heart attack on the first day of practice."

Selena's eyes widened. "Then you'll hire him?"

"Come on," Henry said as he headed for the door. "Let's go down and meet this mysterious Mr. Trader."

When they got down to the field, Trader was surrounded by all the players. One of the behemoths who had tried to tackle him took off his helmet, and Selena blinked when she saw his face. It was Tank Larson, Henry's new star. Without the restrictive helmet, he looked startlingly unthreatening, his sandy hair falling over his forehead and a wide, disarming smile creasing his boyish face. He slapped an arm around Trader's shoulders. "This guy's incredible," Tank yelled at Eli. "Slipped right out from under us." He gave Trader a bearish one-armed hug that actually lifted him off the ground as if he were made of paper. A black player of equal girth ambled over and patted Trader on the back.

"How the dickens did you get away from me?" he asked, his voice filled with admiration.

"Your name's Trader, right?" Tank asked as he made the introductions. "This is Joe Miller, otherwise known as Killer Miller."

Selena watched as Trader made the rounds of introductions, acutely aware of how happy he looked. He was like a grown-up boy playing games with talented kids. An opportunity, she thought. That's all he wanted. Even if he didn't make the team, at least he'd had his moment in the sun on the field today.

"Congratulations," Eli's voice interrupted as he approached the group and warmly shook Trader's hand. "We'll let you stay on a trial basis. Fair enough?"

Trader burst out with a joyous "Yahoo!", all of his anticipation exploding like a firecracker. He rushed around the group, wildly shaking everyone's hand and throwing his arms around his fellow players.

"It's only a trial period," Henry tried to explain, but evidently Trader didn't care.

"It doesn't matter," he explained. "That's all I wanted. I can't thank you enough."

"Don't thank me," Henry said with a knowing glint in his eye. "She's the one to thank." He pointed to Selena, who was still watching shyly from the sidelines.

"Congratulations," she said sincerely. "You got that second chance." She extended her hand, but Trader didn't shake it. Instead, he grabbed her around the waist and lifted her right off her feet. The men all laughed and applauded as she tried to slip out of his grasp, but his arm held her in an iron grip.

"This is for you," he announced exultantly. "For

giving me that second chance."

Before she could stop him, he planted a long and delicious kiss on her mouth, lingering sensually as if they were quite alone, with all the time in the world.

The players all whooped like teenagers, but Selena could have cheerfully strangled him. She wanted at all costs to retain a businesslike demeanor, but she quickly reasoned that to struggle further would only make her look ridiculous. And besides, the shock of his mouth on hers was having a sweetly disturbing effect. He was so blatantly male, the hard lines of his body pressing aggressively against hers. She could tell that the kiss was affecting him as well, because his heart pounded suddenly through the grimy fabric of his jersey.

When he was completely sure that she had surrendered, he lifted his mouth from hers and looked down at her, a devilish glint lighting his clear blue eyes.

"Thanks again," he said huskily. "I appreciate it."

Selena stared at him open-mouthed, fighting the swell of embarrassment.

"I—I don't even know your real name," she stammered.

"That's true, you don't," he answered, looking very pleased with himself. "It's Warren O'Neill," he announced magnanimously, as if he could afford to be generous now that he knew he had made the team. His eyes shone with humor as his hand closed intimately around her waist. "But you can call me Trader."

- 3 -

"HIT THE LIGHTS, would you, Selena?"

Coach Eli finished threading the movie projector while Henry drew the curtains, blocking out the last of the powerful evening sun. As she flicked off the lights in Henry's office high above the stadium, Selena glanced out at the dusky skyline of New York City. She'd never get used to a sun setting over a city instead of a beautifully serene ocean.

The coach turned on the projector, and Selena watched a silver movie of a college football game being played.

"It's an old University of Michigan game!" Henry exclaimed excitedly.

Eli smiled. "I thought you might get a kick out of

that, Henry. Your old alma mater playing its biggest rival, Ohio State."

"Go, big blue!" Henry hollered like a kid in the stands. "When was this game played?"

"Ten years ago. Now watch the screen carefully," Eli said with muted excitement.

Selena leaned forward politely, hiding her inner boredom. Old football movies were not her idea of how to spend an evening.

"Don't mind me if I blank out," she commented. "I've had a long day at the office."

"This might keep you awake," Eli warned. "Watch number eleven."

Something in Eli's voice convinced her to pay attention. She watched the Michigan Wolverines break out of a huddle and line up against their rivals. She paid particular attention to the young man in the number-eleven blue jersey, but could see nothing remarkable.

"Eleven is the quarterback, right?" she asked as she watched the young man on the screen ready himself for the next play.

"Now see if you recognize this play." Eli's voice was low and conspiratorial, as if a great secret were about to be imparted.

The quarterback received the ball and went back to throw a pass, when suddenly two opposing tackles broke through the line and came at him like tanks.

"Throw the ball!" Henry yelled at the screen, as if the endangered number eleven could hear him.

Selena's only thought was of Tank Larson and Killer Miller barreling at Trader that afternoon. She watched curiously, her memory jarred by the disturbing force of the young quarterback's energy. There was something about his lean, compact hips and the way he propelled his body forward with an elegant power that seemed all too familiar. She had seen this predicament before. It was the same, and yet something was different. Her face cringed as she waited for the inevitable onslaught, but it never occurred. With the speed of greased lightning, the young player bolted at the last moment like a tightly wound spring, and shot away from the two gorillas for a sixty-yard run to the end zone.

"Touchdown!" Henry jumped up excitedly. "Boy, that brings back memories! You know, I remember that game."

"You would," Selena couldn't resist saying, but she was still trying to piece it together. The play *had* been remarkable—as remarkable as— She looked at Henry's face suddenly in the light of the projector just as he looked at hers. Then, together, they looked at the screen.

"He repeated that exact play this afternoon down on our field," Eli told them. "Get the picture?"

"Are you sure it's the same guy?" Henry asked.

"It's hard to see his face through his helmet," Selena added, unwilling to believe it.

"Just keep watching," Eli said smugly.

Now at the edge of her seat, Selena watched the game with renewed interest as number eleven performed with incredible agility. Each time he threw the ball, it flew like a guided missile, never missing the arms of its intended receiver. After ten minutes of film, he had completed four passes, and had thrown one of them for a touchdown.

"He's like an eagle," Selena breathed.

"More like a hawk," Henry agreed. "I do remember this game. We were ahead by fourteen points. We should have won easily, but we didn't."

"You mean he lost this game?" Selena frowned. "After a performance like that?"

Henry ignored her as he pieced it all together from memory. "He was definitely pro material," he continued recalling. "I believe the Dallas Cowboys offered him a million-dollar contract."

"Two million," Eli corrected.

Selena's eyes widened. "What happened?"

"He was supposed to play for them after he graduated from college," Henry continued. "O'Neill was a shoe-in."

"Was," Eli emphasized. "Until this next play. Watch."

As Selena looked on, excited and perplexed, the first play, the one she had seen that afternoon on the field, was reenacted. Only this time the agile number eleven slipped on the grass as he tried to bolt from the two huge tackles coming at him. Before he could regain his footing, he was hit hard from the side, his body striking the ground at full force and his helmet thrown violently from his head. Selena found herself bolting up as she saw the face of the young Trader grimace with excruciating pain. Within seconds, three more behemoths were sprawling on top of him.

"My God, they'll kill him!"

"They did," Henry said quietly, his hands involuntarily covering his face.

Sure enough, when the players removed themselves from the pileup, only one was left. There lay

Trader, still wincing in pain as he clutched his knee. Eli hit a switch on the projector, freezing the anguished frame so that it dominated the room, and for a few seconds it was all Selena saw.

Henry shook his head and sighed. "The end of a very promising career."

"Don't be so sure!"

Selena whipped around to see a silhouetted figure stroll casually in front of the screen. Standing with his face only inches from the frozen image on film, he shook his head ruefully.

"What's all this, home movies?" he asked sardonically.

Henry was the first to speak. "You *are* Warren O'Neill?"

"One and the same," Trader confirmed.

"How's the old knee?" Eli asked calmly.

Trader said nothing, but obligingly lifted his trouser leg, revealing no trace of scars or stitches. "I had an arthroscopy."

"Ah." Eli nodded. "A new surgical technique," he explained to Selena and Henry. "Available only in the last few years. I figured as much." He turned back to Trader and eyed him shrewdly. "But I still want to see your medical records as well as X-rays, okay?"

"Should I bring a note from my doctor?" Trader quipped. He looked at Selena through the light of the projector and smiled.

For a moment, she was overcome. Seeing him there next to his image on the screen made her feel as though she had known him all her life, but that was crazy.

"I'll want more than that," Eli continued sternly. "I want you to undergo a complete physical, and that includes some tests of my own. If you can pass muster with me, then, maybe—and only maybe—will you go out on that field."

"Do your worst," Trader acquiesced jovially. He strode to the light switch and illumination flooded the room, dwarfing the frozen image of pain that remained on the screen. Everything about him seemed to radiate a powerful, positive drive—as if he knew this was the one chance he had been waiting for, and he would let nothing get in his way. He caught Selena staring at him and met her gaze with a fully confident grin. His eyes moved casually over her body, as if daring her to interfere, and she caught her breath. The man was always so unnerving. He had come here to ask for something, but his manner was so authoritative that it took all of her resolve to contradict him.

"Are you sure you're in shape?" she asked awkwardly, fumbling for anything to say in order to avoid the tension that had sprung up between them. She wondered nervously if Eli or Henry could tell, but they were looking at Trader, not at her.

"I intend to be hard on you," Eli warned.

Apparently, Trader wasn't at all fazed. Leaning back against the wall, he folded his arms casually, but the easy grin disappeared from his angular features. "Go ahead," he said, looking Eli straight in the eye. "I've already beaten you to the punch. Every day I do a fifteen-mile run, one hundred push-ups, two hundred sit-ups, an hour in the weight room, and another hour of practice with the football. Try me."

"Humph," was all Eli could say.

But Selena was filled with admiration. She didn't care what Eli or Henry thought. Trader was like a moving force that couldn't be stopped. His lean, powerful body lounged against the wall as if he didn't have a care in the world, but she knew instinctively that he was going to play football again, and that he was going to play for the Aces. He had already won. Henry looked at her to see what she was thinking, but her gaze was still riveted on Trader.

"A trial basis," Henry announced finally. He shook his head as he thought about the prospects. "I still don't like the age factor, but for the moment, until I can get more capital together for a quarterback, you're all we've got."

Eli grimaced. "I expect to see you down here tomorrow, an hour ahead of the rest of the team. I'm going to work you till you drop."

"And if I don't drop?" Trader challenged. He walked to the doorway and turned to await Eli's answer.

"You'll drop," Eli said humorlessly. "Trust me."

"See you tomorrow, coach," Trader saluted him, and was about to leave when he acknowledged Selena, who was still staring at him in awe. "Thanks again for my second chance," he said to her in a low, velvety voice. For a moment, it seemed as if there were an invisible line between them, connecting them effortlessly on the same wavelength. But then he was gone.

The door closed with a little click, leaving only the lingering image on the screen.

"He'll drop," Eli repeated. "Trust me. He'll drop."

Selena shook her head, still caught under Trader's spell. "Don't be so sure." Suddenly, she knew without a doubt that Trader was going to get everything he wanted, and moreover, that he had planned it all in advance. She had the uncanny feeling that all of them had been playing right into his hands. Before Henry could stop her, she jumped up and followed Trader out the door, looking down the deserted hallway toward the sound of his faint footsteps.

"Trader!" she called, her voice echoing through the cool, concrete corridors. "Hey! Wait up!" Total silence followed, and she looked around uncertainly. "Now where did he go?"

"Right behind you."

She jumped as his unseen hands came around from behind, resting on her shoulders.

"Tense," he commented briefly as his fingers settled on the soft skin of her neck. "Definitely overworked." Slowly, irresistibly, his strong fingers began a subtle massage.

"You scared me," she gulped, trying to pretend that his touch was not affecting her the way it was. Each firm, blessed stroke was sending a shaft of warm pleasure through her tired body. And the sense of relief created by the massage was tempered by the uprush of desire that was building at the end of each well-placed rub.

"Here?" he guessed, hitting a particularly tense area. His knowing hands worked her shoulder blades, shooting a ripple of gladness through her.

Selena could barely speak. She nodded weakly. "Where—where did you ever learn to do that?"

"It comes with the territory." She couldn't see his face, but somehow she just knew that he was grinning confidently at the depth of her response.

His hands moved to another spot, and her eyes closed helplessly.

"So how's the paper-box industry treating you these days?" he asked teasingly.

A telltale muscle in her back jumped with tension when he said that, and she tried in vain to hide it.

"Relax, Selena," he whispered. "You're too up-tight."

"I can't help it. It's this city," she lied, groping for an excuse. "It—it does that to people. Where I come from, the pace is a lot slower."

"I believe the word for that is 'mellow,' am I right?" His arms came around her and held her lightly. It should have seemed strange to be standing so intimately in the hallway with him, but she knew how inevitably this moment had been building between them. She had known it ever since that first day in the bar when the magical persuasion of tequila had melted her inhibitions and told her exactly how much she wanted this man. And how much he wanted her.

His head bent slightly, and his nose brushed against her neck. It was a small gesture but a very intimate one, and something in Selena snapped as she whirled in his arms to face him. For a second, nothing happened, and then everything happened as her tilted chin gave him the invitation he sought. Their lips met in a silken rush of energy, charging them both with delicious new feelings of sensuality.

"Mmm," Trader murmured when the kiss broke. "I knew you would be this sweet."

Selena looked into his steely blue eyes, wondering how it could feel so natural to be kissing Trader O'Neill in the stadium hall after hours. "It's funny," she said slowly, "but I feel as if I've known you all my life, as if we'd met before."

"Who knows? Anything is possible. But I think we should do some more research to be sure." Trader pulled her close and kissed her again. This time the kiss was fused with deliberate passion instead of the breathlessness of discovery. The flames began to dance and swirl inside of her, licking and teasing every nerve-ending in her body. Time was lost to her as she gave herself up to the sweet oblivion, and she realized in a flash how right this felt. She had no qualms about what she was doing. The spark between her and Trader had burst into fire, and now there was no going back.

Unexpectedly, he pushed away from her abruptly. Still flushed with passion, she fluttered open her eyes, confused. "What—what is it?" she murmured.

He frowned and shook his head, and her heart dropped. "This isn't right," he said sternly. "I don't like the way this looks."

Selena didn't care how it looked. She and Henry had never meddled in each other's private lives, and as for Eli—well, he was nobody's fool. Besides, it was simply none of his business.

"What isn't right?" she asked reluctantly, knowing already what he would say.

"Everything. I can't make love to you, Selena, as much as I would like to."

That threw her. "Who said anything about making love?" she countered evenly.

He let out an impatient breath. "Well, that's what kissing generally leads to."

"It's a far cry from a few kisses to—to jumping into bed!" she cried, torn between her hidden disappointment that he wasn't going to at least try, and her anger at the high-handedness of his one-sided decision.

"Look, Selena, I just don't want anyone to think that I slept my way onto the team. I've worked so hard for this chance. It's important that I make it on my own merit and that nothing else get in the way."

"Then why did you creep up on me like this?" she demanded, her face reddening. "Why did you start this?"

"Because it's inevitable," he said bluntly, his magnificent eyes raking her body disturbingly. "But the timing just isn't right."

"Oh." She could think of nothing else to say, but she nodded several times in mock agreement. "I see you have it all figured out."

"It's my fault," he said, softening. For a moment, she thought he would take her in his arms again, but although his eyes seemed to glow with longing, he merely stood there and looked at her. "I'm sorry," he added. "Look, I know I owe you a lot."

"You don't owe me anything."

"Ah, but I do. If it weren't for you, I wouldn't have had a chance of getting even a tryout."

"I'm not so sure about that." She fumbled with a pleat in her dress and looked everywhere else but at him.

"Come on," he announced, breaking into her unease. "Let's celebrate, boss. I'm going to take you to the best restaurant in New York." Before she could protest, he was escorting her out of the stadium and over to a sports car that was parked in the huge, vacant lot.

Selena said nothing, but climbed into the small car with a hint of a smile. Trader was fooling himself, of that much she was sure. Dinner would only serve to heighten the flames that seemed to leap up and entwine them whenever they were together. But sometimes a leisurely, tantalizing approach was the best. Now that she knew how she felt about him, now that her own longing was out in the open, she had every intention of seeing it through.

The car had that leathery, outdoors smell that only very new cars have, and she looked around appreciatively as she settled into the bucket seat. Well, at least he's not poor, she thought wryly as she touched the seat with one finger. She looked around furtively for more clues as to who Trader O'Neill really was, but saw nothing except for a copy of *The Wall Street Journal* and a small notepad with meaningless figures on it.

Trader drove swiftly and confidently, handling the snarled traffic as if it were second nature to him. They said nothing to each other during the brief drive, but the silence was companionable. Selena waited patiently, knowing that the chemistry between them would eventually win out.

"Here's the turnoff," he said after several minutes had passed. "We'll be at the Duchess's in no time at all. She's only a couple of blocks from the Brooklyn Bridge."

Selena turned in her seat, impressed. "The Duchess?" she repeated. "You do travel in fancy circles, don't you?" She looked down at her business suit. "I hope this is all right to wear."

"What? Oh, don't worry about that. The Duchess is anything but chic." He laughed heartily, and Selena frowned. She could never be sure exactly what he was up to, and this time she knew she was in for a surprise.

Trader grinned mysteriously as they pulled off the expressway, turning down a dark street right under the Brooklyn Bridge. At the end of the block, he made an extreme right turn onto a dead-end street that was paved with cobblestones. A row of run-down Victorian brownstones lined both sides of the block. In front of one particularly shabby building, an old-fashioned gas lamp cast a ghostly light on the quiet scene.

"This is spooky," Selena whispered as Trader switched off the engine. She looked around for a restaurant sign, but there was none.

Trader opened the door for her, but Selena hesitated before emerging from the car. "Is it safe around here?" she asked dubiously.

"Safest place in Brooklyn," he assured her. "The Duchess wouldn't have it any other way."

"Who is this Duchess, anyway?" Selena asked suspiciously. This certainly wasn't anything like Los Angeles. There wasn't a soul in sight. Just a few parked cars.

"The Duchess," Trader explained, "is the sweetest old lady you'd ever want to know. And she has the best soul-food restaurant in the world."

He headed for the shabby house with the gaslight and walked down a short flight of steps that led to a door. Suddenly, a window on the top floor was flung open, making Selena gasp with alarm.

"What the hell you think you're doing down there, mister?" The voice was harsh and defiant, daring them to take another step. Selena squinted up and saw that it belonged to an old black woman who was glaring down at them. Her silhouette was large and round and she held a ladle in her hand as though she might actually use it on someone's head.

Selena grabbed Trader's arm. "Let's get out of here.

I know a nice Italian restaurant on Second Avenue and—"

"You got yourself just two seconds to git afore I pour hot water out this window."

"I think she means business," Selena warned, but her retreat was stopped by Trader's arm. He laughed aloud as if he was thoroughly enjoying himself, and then shook his finger up at the old woman in the window.

"Is that any way to treat your best customer?" he asked, holding Selena firmly against him.

"Who is that?" The old woman peered down and let out a short, biting laugh. "Why, Trader, you young hoot, I thought you was some bum off the street. Just a second, I'll come down and let y'all in."

"Who is she?" Selena asked Trader as they waited in front of the door.

Trader chuckled. "Haven't you figured it out yet, Selena? That's the Duchess."

- 4 -

IT TOOK A few minutes before Selena could hear the woman's footsteps coming down the stairs, but there was no mistaking them when she did. Each one seemed to shake the old house with its massive weight, and she clung to Trader as they waited. They listened as one bolt was undone, followed by a second and a third. Selena heard the final chain being slid aside and a bar being removed, and she wondered frantically what she was doing here at all.

"Is she afraid of someone getting in—or out?" she managed to quip before the ancient door swung open to reveal the rotund, gaily dressed woman who let out a whoop when she saw Trader.

Selena stared. The woman was wearing a flowered

dress from the forties, and her hair was covered by a large bandanna that was tied tightly behind one ear. Huge gold hoops dangled from both ears, and they danced around her face as she threw her arms open. Before anyone could say a word, she wrapped her arms around Trader and kissed him resoundingly on both cheeks.

"How are you, Duchess?" he asked warmly. "It's been too long."

"My, my, how time does fly," she answered, patting him solidly on the cheek. She took a step back. "Let me get a good look at you, now." Her brilliant smile faded into a pout. "You been taking off weight, honey? It's about time you came round. I'm fixing to fatten you up."

"I went into training, and your food became off-limits," he explained with sincere regret. Then he smiled broadly and clapped his hands. "But tonight I'm celebrating, and the sky's the limit."

"Well," the Duchess announced firmly, "come on up and set yourselves down." Trader bounded after her, but Selena hesitated.

"You, too, honey," the Duchess added, turning her commanding gaze on Selena. "You'll catch your death of cold out there."

Selena stepped in and watched as the Duchess re-fastened all the bolts on the door, securing everything back in place.

"Is all that necessary?" Selena asked cautiously. She got no answer at all, and they marched up the stairs in a single row.

"You like corn bread?" Trader asked. "Because the Duchess makes the best corn bread on earth."

Selena was too overwhelmed to answer. She gave him a "you-got-me-into-this" look and bravely continued climbing the next flight.

They were escorted into what had once been an elegant drawing room, now converted into a restaurant. There were six tables in all, and Selena was surprised to see three of them occupied by guests who were busily engaged in eating heartily. An old upright piano sat in the very center of the room, holding a vase of fresh roses. As they passed it, Selena saw a yellowed piece of sheet music perched on top and her eyes widened as she caught the title: "Satin Doll" by Duke Ellington, with the Duke's original signature on the bottom.

"Is this for real?" she whispered as they were seated at an old wooden table with chairs whose legs had seen better days. Selena's chair rocked back and forth of its own accord.

"I hope she's serving fried potato skins," Trader enthused, as excited as a child waiting for a birthday present. "Her yams melt in your mouth. And her crab apples—"

Two plates were slapped on the table in front of them, causing Selena to sit up with a bolt. A basket of steaming corn bread followed instantly, along with a plate of sweet butter.

"Chicken Crawdaddy tonight," the Duchess announced abruptly, in her no-nonsense tone. "I got an apple betty for dessert and crab apple compote."

"Uh—could I see a menu, please?" Selena asked politely. "I think I might like an appetizer, and—"

The Duchess threw her a look that froze the words in her mouth. "We ain't got no menu. You'll eat

Chicken Crawdaddy, 'cause that's what I'm serving. This ain't Fifth Avenue, you know." She turned back to Trader and gave him a honeyed smile. "Got something special for you tonight, sugar. Baked yams with marshmallow."

Selena beamed in relief. "I'll have that, too. It sounds great."

"I just told you," the Duchess said impatiently. "You're having chicken. I know what's best. Don't meddle with me." And she marched off in a huff, back to the kitchen.

Selena stared after her. "If that isn't the rudest—" She reached for a slice of corn bread and buttered it angrily. "Is this supposed to be some kind of delightful local color? Because if it is," she added, taking a bite of the corn bread, "you'd think she could at least—" Suddenly, her eyes lit up and she looked at the corn bread for the first time. "Wow," she pronounced, "this is heavenly. It's actually melting in my mouth." She devoured the rest of the slice, unabashedly licking the butter from her fingers.

Trader smiled knowingly. "Wait till you taste the chicken."

Selena couldn't answer; she was too busy stuffing another piece of corn bread into her mouth.

"Best food in the world," Trader said. "The absolute best."

"How did you ever find this crazy place?" Selena asked between bites.

"One of my clients told me about it. Only a handful of people know about it, and some who do aren't allowed in. The Duchess is very picky about her customers."

Selena could believe it, but the mention of his business piqued her curiosity even more. "And who are your clients?" she asked, trying to sound casual.

"People with a lot of money who count on me for advice." His tone was just as casual, except that she could tell *he* wasn't faking it. He took a piece of corn bread and ate it with relish.

"And who are *your* clients?" he asked after a moment.

"Mostly manufacturers. You know, businesses that need to put their products in boxes." It sounded painfully obvious after she said it, and she stifled a frown.

"Sounds exciting," Trader said dryly. "How'd you get hoodwinked into that business?"

"Who said anything about hoodwinked? It was my father's company and—"

"And you felt you owed it to him to carry on the tradition, right?"

"Something like that."

He shook his head and smiled sardonically. "What about buying the Aces?" he pressed.

"That was Henry's idea." She sighed. Trader's eyes twinkled sympathetically, and she felt compelled to continue. "It was what he wanted. I didn't really object exactly, but I didn't have any alternatives lined up."

"You're very agreeable," Trader observed.

"I know," she said ruefully. "I can't say no to Henry. In fact, I have trouble saying no to anyone." She looked down, sorry she had revealed that last truth, but Trader laughed gently.

"If you cared passionately about the company," he said, "you would have found it easy to say no. What amazes me, though, is that in spite of everything, you're very good at what you do." He reached out and toyed with the dolphin pendant hanging from her necklace.

Selena was genuinely surprised. "Why—thank you. That's the first real compliment you've given me."

His hand let go of the pendant and touched hers. Their eyes locked and she felt a strange stirring inside of her. Somehow Trader was looking effortlessly through her polished outer layers and seeing the vulnerability underneath. He had done that ever since she had known him, and for the first time she found herself not only attracted to him but wanting him to unravel her even more. It wasn't just that the company had become more of a burden than a challenge. That much was true, although Trader was the only person in her life who had been able to see it. It was that she wasn't sure what could replace it, and she had kept going in an effort to forestall any kind of decision or change.

She had the distinct feeling that he read all of her conflicting emotions in her eyes, and her hand closed around his. The one gesture was strangely intimate, as if they were suddenly quite alone in the room. Trader's eyes softened to a deep, liquid blue, and Selena was aware that her mouth had parted breathlessly in an unspoken invitation.

But the moment was shattered mercilessly as the Duchess reappeared, bearing two plates, which she practically threw down on the table in front of them.

"Here you go, honey," she drawled. "Just don't let this sweet-talker sell you anything more than you can afford to lose."

The Duchess gave Trader a fond smile, patted him

on the back, and sashayed over to the piano. She sat down and began playing an old blues arrangement, quietly humming to herself.

Selena was startled, but she was getting used to being startled in this place. "If this isn't the strangest restaurant I've ever eaten at," she mumbled, looking down at the plate in front of her. The Chicken Crawdaddy was spicy and colorful, giving off a savory aroma that was like nothing she had ever smelled before. It was accompanied by southern-style green beans and a fluffy mound of yams covered with marshmallows. "Well, look at that," she said, surprised. "She gave me the yams after all."

Trader smiled. "She's all bark and no bite. Well, almost no bite. Would you like something to drink?"

Selena nodded hungrily. "What do you think she'll let me have?"

He laughed heartily. "Say, Duchess?" he called, but the hostess ignored him and went right on playing the piano. "Uh, Duchess?"

"I hear you. My ears still work, thank the Lord."

"Do you think you could manage a little wine?"

"I could," the Duchess answered, "but not right now. These feet done too much standing today. And these old fingers need a little exercise on this here piano. You want wine, you know where it is."

Selena gave up and tried the food. As she had anticipated, it was spectacular. "Is she always like this?" she asked curiously.

"Oh, yes." Trader nodded, heading resignedly into the kitchen for the wine while Selena listened to the Duchess play.

"You got to watch out for that man," the Duchess

sang in a raw alto as she looked haughtily in Selena's direction. "Watch out he don't use you. 'Cause that man is a stranger to your heart." As she hummed a few more bars, she added the last few words to end the song. "'Cause that man come out of nowhere to steal your heart."

Selena pretended to look away while Trader returned. "Here's the wine," he announced above the sultry chords of the piano. He placed the carafe of white wine down and poured two glasses.

Selena decided to concentrate on the food, which turned out to be the best possible decision. She forgot everything as the Duchess's flavorful and satisfying cooking wove its magic. It wasn't just that the food was expertly prepared, with unusual and effective combinations of color and texture and taste. The ingredients were completely fresh, and there was a wholesome, honest quality to everything, truly giving the effect of a home-cooked meal.

Conversation between them waned for a few minutes, for which Selena was glad. It was almost a relief to have Trader's soul-searching eyes trained on something else for a while. The Duchess continued to spin slow, seductive tunes on the old piano, only stopping long enough to take a tray of apple betty from the kitchen and dole out portions to all the diners. The music continued, weaving a spell around them as the night lengthened.

"'Satin Doll,'" Selena murmured, recognizing a tune. "I love that song."

"Care to dance?"

Before she could say no, Trader had her out on the old wooden floor. He took her slowly into his arms, the floor creaking with each step. The setting was anything but elegant, and yet somehow it was one of the most romantic sensations Selena had ever experienced. Trader held her intimately, one hand resting on her hip, the other on her back, and time fell away from them as they swayed lazily to one jazzy tune after another.

They were in a fantasy world that existed only for them. The stirrings of desire licked at their senses, but neither wanted to end the magic. Selena rested her head on Trader's shoulder, but every now and then she looked up to see the pleasure in his eyes, and they would exchange a deep, silent, private look.

He smiled when the Duchess began to play "Happy Talk," a show tune from *South Pacific*, but she gave it a slow, bluesy treatment that transformed it into a sly, sensual song. Selena listened dreamily, her heart beating against the strong, hard wall of Trader's chest. The words at the end of the refrain were about the necessity of having dreams, and making those dreams come true.

She could feel the vitality coursing through Trader, filtering through the haze of relaxation, and she realized how excited he was at what had happened today. Playing football was deeply, crucially important to him, she thought with a stab of envy. How wonderful it must be to care about something so much.

"Your dream has come true for you, hasn't it?" she whispered.

"We all need to have dreams." Trader echoed the sentiments of the song as the Duchess sang the closing lines over again. He held her closer and they danced the final notes away.

"What's your dream, Selena?" he asked as the Duchess finished the song.

She had no answer. All she could do was stare up at him in awe. Their eyes locked, and she felt a surge of triumph as she knew that he was about to kiss her. His face drew near, and then they both jumped as the Duchess shut the piano with a loud bang.

"That's it, folks. Quitting time. The Duchess needs her beauty sleep. So, pay up and haul out."

Selena gulped and managed a weak laugh as Trader paid the check and escorted her down the flights of steps and out into the cool evening. She didn't want it to be over, not yet. "How about a nightcap somewhere else?" she suggested, but Trader shook his head.

"Sorry, I'm in training now. Early to bed and early to rise. Come on. I'll drive you back to your car at the stadium."

The unwelcome reality intruded unpleasantly into the remainder of the evening, and Selena couldn't hide her disappointment as he drove swiftly back to the stadium. Trader had sworn that he would stay uninvolved with her as long as he still needed to prove himself to the team, and it looked as if he was bound and determined to stick to that plan. He helped her out of the car in a courtly fashion, and escorted her over to her own car.

"I hope you enjoyed it," he said rather formally.

Selena blinked. How had things become so removed all of a sudden? Was it because he knew all too well where the evening would lead if he let his guard down now? She hid a smirk and looked up at him innocently. "Oh, I did," she said earnestly. Her hands touched his arms, reviving the sparks of desire that had been building and teasing them all through the dancing at the Duchess's, and she looked up into his eyes.

She knew he wanted to kiss her, knew it as surely as a flame finds dry tinder. But he only stood there, his face at war with itself, gazing down at her with a longing that went straight to her heart.

There was only one thing to do. She stood on her toes, took his face gently in her hands, and kissed him with a slow and tantalizing sense of discovery. A tingle of response, like the ringing of a thousand tiny bells, shot through her, but she did not pursue what she had begun. Instead, she remained in his arms, her face only inches from his and her eyes half closed, as she savored the lingering sweetness that had claimed her.

"Mmm," she whispered softly, reinforcing the pleasure that had enveloped them. Then she let herself down, ran her hands lightly down his chest in a gesture of farewell, and slipped quietly to her car.

Although Selena never would have admitted it, Trader's effect on her life was like a pebble being thrown into a still morning lake. The tiny ripple created a series of waves that scampered out in all directions. No one noticed the change in her, but, imperceptibly, little things began to happen. A week after her impromptu dinner with Trader, Selena threw down her gold pen and realized with a slight sense of horror that she actually felt restless—even bored— for the first time since she had taken over the reins at Derringer Industries. What had once been so fulfilling now seemed to be exactly what Trader had said it was—the unexciting marketing of corrugated boxes. It was maddening that he could have been so right, but during a marketing meeting in which a new design for a blister-pack machine was being unveiled, Selena caught herself doodling jewelry designs—something she hadn't done for almost three years.

Late that night, unable to sleep, she was suddenly struck by something they had talked about. At three in the morning, she got out of bed and dragged a dilapidated Derringer box from the back of the closet. It contained an assortment of jewelry tools she had brought with her from L. A., mementos she had never been able to bring herself to throw away. She opened it slowly, greeting the worn tools like old friends, and she sat with them until dawn. She had no idea what she was going to do with them. Perhaps it was just a bit of nostalgia—even homesickness—that had haunted her in the night. But it was impossible to deny that Trader had been the cause of her silent ennui, and suddenly she wanted to see him again, to confront him with the results of his needling.

That was not so easy to do. Trader was impossible to reach. Eli kept him so busy that everything she heard about him came secondhand from Henry, who now spent his entire workday at the stadium. According to the grapevine, Trader was being totally reconditioned. He now lived, ate, and breathed nothing but football.

"He's incredible, Selena," Henry raved as they rode in the newly acquired Derringer limousine that Henry had purchased for chauffeuring his players around to various press conferences. "You'd think he just got out of college. The guy throws a football like a guided missile. He never misses a shot."

Selena was only half listening. She was too uncomfortable scrunched between Tank Larson and Killer Miller, who managed to take up three seats between them. They had just come from a press conference where Henry had announced his plans to build five thousand additional seats at the stadium. To accomplish this, he had sold another three percent of his Derringer stocks, which gave Selena the controlling interest.

"Yeah," Tank agreed, stirring Selena out of her reverie. "That guy's like greased lightning. One minute I got a hold on him, and the next—" Tank opened his hand, palms up, as if to show that nothing was in them. One of his hands alone looked as if it could crush a bowling ball, and Selena shuddered to think what it could do to Trader. She looked across where Henry sat opposite all of them, comfortably sipping a lemonade. Now was definitely not a good time to tell her brother that she was secretly planning to sell the Aces. Especially not with these two monsters surrounding her.

"I never saw a happier guy, though," Killer added. "You can't get a rise out him. He's just happy playing football."

Oh, brother, Selena said to herself, frowning. To think she would be breaking two hearts at once. Henry would lose his precious team, and Trader would undoubtedly be dropped for younger blood, no matter how good he was now. She let out a heavy sigh as she contemplated the delicate and complex work she faced before the major stockholders' meeting in two weeks. That meeting would be doomsday for Henry, and for Trader.

The limousine pulled into the stadium parking lot.

"Back to the old grind," Killer said good-naturedly as he opened the door and stepped out. A rush of air revived Selena's crushed ribs. She emerged from the car and headed into the coolness of the stadium. Through the long tunnel leading to the stands, she could see, as if through a telescope, a part of the field. A lone player stood with his hands on his hips, staring through his helmet across the field, the number eleven painted brightly on his blue jersey.

Selena couldn't believe how glad she was to see him. The unexpected pleasure rushed through her, bringing color to her cheeks. "Hello," she called out to him, but he didn't so much as turn. "Hey, Trader!"

He whipped around and Selena started to wave, but he wasn't watching her. He was racing to catch an overthrown ball. She watched as he leaped three feet in the air and easily caught the ball in one hand as naturally as a hawk would catch a falling object. Never had she seen a man so much in his element. Watching Trader on the field was like watching a ballerina at the high point of a performance or a lion loping across the jungle.

His sprint slowed as he approached her, and she realized that he had become aware of her presence. "Hi," she said shyly.

"How's it going, Selena?" he panted gruffly, addressing her like one of the guys.

"Is that really you, Trader?" She glared through his faceplate. An inch of black paste was smeared under each eye, making him look like a monster from a grade-B movie. She poked a finger through the protective visor and touched one of the black marks.

"It's used to catch the dirt and keep it from getting

into your eyes," he explained, amused.

"The smell of the greasepaint and the roar of the crowd," she mused. Trader laughed and took off his helmet, standing boyishly with his head cocked to one side. His face was glowing with good health and vitality, and she wanted to put her arms around him right there on the field. She had never seen another human being look so happy in her life, and she found that his joy was oddly contagious. "You're looking good," she ventured jauntily.

His eyes traveled over her candidly. "So are you."

"I haven't heard from you," she stated point-blank.

"I know." He grinned. "Eli is a real slave driver, but I get a day off soon. You know what we both need?" She shook her head breathlessly, completely caught up in his enthusiasm. "We should get out and head to this crazy little Egyptian place I know down in SoHo. It's down in a basement and it doesn't have any tables or chairs. You just sit on the floor. And the—"

"Wait a minute," she broke in archly. "What about your noble resolve to stay away from me?"

"Well, we both have to eat, don't we?" he objected sensibly. He began walking her off the field, but stopped when he caught the triumphant glint in her eye. "Don't toy with me, Selena. I've got a commitment right now that won't stop for anyone or anything. But when I'm ready," he added, his eyes raking her over meaningfully, "you'll be ready for me. That I guarantee."

Selena continued walking, looking straight ahead to avoid his eyes. His passion for football might be the driving force in his life, but he certainly knew how to ignite her when he wanted to. She wondered fleetingly if he would ever really have time for her, but the doubt was overshadowed by the much bigger problem of her intention to sell the team. Trader would be crushed, that was obvious. And he would never forgive her. The guilt settled into her, nestling deeply and uncomfortably in her heart, and she was unaware that Trader was watching her like a hawk.

"Don't pout," he goaded her cheerfully. "I'm just teasing you, Selena."

"No, you're not," she mumbled, recalling his bold words. "You meant every word."

"I'm impossible, aren't I?" he agreed in the same maddeningly cheerful tone. She stole a glance at him and saw once again the unquenchable happiness that shone all over his face. "Look, what about dinner?" he pressed.

"On the floor?" she countered. "It sounds sort of strange, Trader. Don't you ever go any place normal?"

He frowned thoughtfully. "Oh, I guess so. But normal is so boring." Then he brightened. "I could take you up to my place in the Berkshires," he suggested. "Is that normal enough for you?"

It was Selena's turn to frown. "Definitely not platonic enough," she said demurely. "Besides," she added seriously, "I can't leave town. I've got the stockholders' meeting coming up, and there's a ton of work to do. I may have to work straight through the weekend."

"All work and no play makes Selena a dull girl." He leaned against the railing of the stands and folded his arms as if expecting her to change her mind. She perceived that Trader O'Neill wasn't used to taking no for an answer, and immediately she decided to change that record.

"Playing football all day makes Trader a dull boy," she retorted.

"You call this kind of training *play?*"

"No," Selena answered, "just dull."

"This from a lady who spends her days thinking about paper boxes," he taunted.

"And you suggest I liven up by eating on the floor?" she asked dryly.

"Not necessarily," he said, squinting down at her. "Maybe you should become a cheerleader for the Aces."

"What?" Selena practically choked. "What hat did you pull that out of? Are you crazy?"

"Why not?" he continued, ignoring her outrage. "It would be fun, and undoubtedly good for you. You need something to root for, Selena, something to lose yourself in. Something crazy and fun and not too serious. Besides," he added with a cheeky grin, "I bet you'd look great in one of those cheerleader outfits."

"No thanks." Selena laughed, assuming uneasily that he was kidding. "I've got my work cut out for me at Derringer. And it doesn't include prancing half-dressed around a football field. Besides," she added flippantly, "I may be moving up of my own accord."

He stared at her intently for a few seconds, as if analyzing and dissecting everything she had just said. It was as if he could read her mind, and Selena had an irrational urge to shield her eyes from that unyielding gaze. There were things going on in her mind that she definitely did not want him to know about, and no sixth sense of his was going to penetrate her resolve. His eyes narrowed suddenly and she nearly flinched.

"The only way you can move up," he said finally, "would be to take over Henry's position as chairman of the board. But if you're planning any interesting moves," he said finally, "I'd like to know about them."

She answered him with complete silence, wanting to kick herself for saying as much as she had. The company's business was just that—the Derringers' business and no one else's.

His seriousness fell away with a sudden deliberation, and he favored her with a careless grin. Thankfully, he wasn't going to pursue it. "Well," he said amiably, "you shouldn't be working so hard. It's not good for you."

"Sorry," she said. "But I'm taking a meeting this afternoon at four and after that I've got to face the year's financial statements."

Trader burst into laughter. "You're what?" he demanded. "Taking a meeting?" He kept on laughing as if it were the funniest thing he had ever heard.

"And what's so funny about that?" she asked irritably. Trader's unpredictability sometimes made her dizzy.

"Listen, California girl," he explained between chuckles. "You're in New York now. And in New York, no one *takes* a meeting. We simply *have* a meeting. The only thing you take in this city is a taxi *to* the meeting or an aspirin *after* the meeting or a cup of coffee *during* the meeting. Got it?"

Selena refused to go along with him. "Are you making fun of me?"

"Don't take it so seriously, California girl; we all have our faults."

"As in San Andreas, right?" she couldn't resist asking.

Trader grinned. "You said it, not I."

"O'Neill!" Eli shouted authoritatively.

"Oops!" Trader straightened up at once. "Got to go." He blew her a kiss, put on his helmet, and ran to rejoin the team.

"Boys will be boys," she muttered to herself, feeling relief that their edgy encounter had ended and a strange sense of anticipation.

The truth surfaced cleanly in her heart as she watched him. So many things were about to come to a head. It was only a matter of time.

- 5 -

SELENA WAS ALL business as she strode through the corridors of Derringer's new offices that afternoon. Her mind was buzzing with the two earth-shaking tasks ahead of her: She had to take over as chairman of the board, and she had to sell the Aces. No small ambition, but she had grown used to making hair-raising decisions ever since the Aces had become part of her life. There was no doubt in her mind that once the Aces were removed, things would get back to normal.

She was so intent on her thoughts that she didn't see a huge pile of folded flat boxes piled to the ceiling. As she made her turn around the sleek corridor, she ran smack into them, sending the entire load scattering out over the floor like an unruly deck of gigantic playing cards.

Several employees' heads popped out of offices to see the boss standing there among the mess, and they all came fluttering to help clean it up like so many busy bees buzzing around the queen.

"Are you all right, Ms. Derringer?"

"Don't worry, Ms. Derringer; I'll clean it up."

"We'll take care of it, Ms. Derringer."

"Terrific," she said, waving her hand in thanks. She was barely listening. She continued barreling down the hall, still so bent on her own thoughts that she narrowly missed another pile as she headed into her office.

"Barry," she said to the earnest young man who guarded her fortress. "Send a memo out to everyone. I don't want any more piles of boxes sitting out in the hall. We have a warehouse for that."

"Uh, Selena," Barry tried to put in, "there's a man waiting to see you who just stormed past my desk—"

"My God," Selena interrupted him, "now I know how those football players feel dodging those huge tackles."

"Oh, do you, now?"

Selena stopped cold at the sound of that by-now all-too-familiar voice, and surveyed her empty office. "Trader?" Looking around, she saw no one. "Where are you?"

Slowly, the big leather chair behind her desk turned. There he was, dressed in jeans and a University of Michigan jersey, lounging comfortably. She clamped her lips together, determined not to lose her cool.

Trader always made that difficult. He managed to look rakishly sensual in her big chair, as if he had just climbed out of a romp in bed.

"Trying it out for size?" Selena quipped. She didn't want Barry to see her consternation, but the young man was very perceptive. He backed diplomatically out of the office, closing the door with a little click.

"Yes," Trader answered her. "How do I look as chairman of the board of Derringer Industries?" He laced his hands behind his head and beamed up at her.

"Terrific image," Selena said dryly. "That's all this company needs, a football player as CEO."

"Aah," he raised a finger up at her, "but I'm no ordinary player. You forget, I'm the quarterback."

"So?" She was beginning to lose patience. There was so much work to do, and the sudden ringing of the phone made her jump. Barry picked it up on his end, and when he did not buzz her, she knew he had told the caller that she was in a meeting. Trader had never had the opportunity to accurately see her business side. It was high time he found out. "Look, Trader," she said sternly, "if you want to see me, you'll have to make an appointment."

"I know, I know," he said mildly. "You've got big shots cooling their heels out there waiting to see you, right?"

"Something like that." She met his bold stare evenly. "So get lost."

"But I can help you, Selena." His blue eyes seemed to sparkle with invitation. "The quarterback calls all the plays, remember? I've got the perfect credentials for running this company."

"Is that so?" she asked faintly.

"Would you like to see my résumé?"

Suddenly, she'd had enough. Striding over to her chair, she jerked a thumb toward the door. "I mean it, Trader, I've got work to do. You can't just—"

He ignored her protest and grabbed her wrist, swinging her around so that she landed squarely on his lap.

"What are you doing?" she cried, struggling against him. "What if Barry—"

"This," he said huskily, and immediately planted a long, luscious kiss on her open mouth. He held her firmly in his strong grip, and although she tried her very best to stop the rising tide of response, it was no use. The flutter of desire grew into a coiled spring ready to consume her. Lord, but the man had a stunning effect on her, she realized soberly when the kiss ended. All he had to do was touch her and she was lost. No wonder he had vowed to stay away from her. Together they were like a burning fuse.

"What was that for?" she whispered against his shoulder. "I thought you were committed to avoiding involvement with me." She thought it was a rhetorical question, but he surprised her with a ready answer.

"That was last week," he said cheerfully, dropping sensual, warm kisses on her face, her neck, her throat.

"And this week?" she squirmed breathlessly, drinking in the delicious sensation even as she threw a quick glance at the doorway to make sure Barry wasn't able to hear anything.

"This week things are different. Eli has worked me to death, and yesterday he finally threw in the towel. He agrees I've proven my worth as a quarterback, and so—" He grinned mischievously and spun them both around in the chair a few times. "So, now I'm free to pursue another interest."

She shook her head. "Sorry to disappoint you, Trader, but you seem to be good at making unilateral decisions."

"What?"

"Meaning that *you* may have decided to come marching in here and monopolize my time, but you are the only one who has agreed to it. Haven't you ever heard of mutual consent?"

He sighed impatiently. "Don't give me that, Selena. Last week you were ready and interested. And you practically melted in my arms just now. I warn you, honey, don't play games with me."

"You seem to be the expert game player here," she retorted, stung. "You call all the shots, don't you? You decide when I'm supposed to fall into your arms, right?"

He grinned. "I told you, I'm the quarterback. That's my job."

"Not with me, it's not." She jumped off his lap before he could stop her and perched safely on the edge of her desk. "I've got so much work to finish here that I can't begin to think of anything else. I'll probably be here all weekend," she added, looking down worriedly at the mound of papers on her desk.

He frowned slightly and followed her gaze. "You worry too much, Selena. Don't take everything so seriously. There probably isn't as much here as you think. If you let me help you, I'll bet we can both get out of here before the weekend."

"But that's ridiculous," she said. "You don't know anything about my business."

His eyes twinkled. "Maybe I know more than you think. Let's make a deal, Selena. Let me pitch in, and I say we can have everything finished before the end of the day. If I'm right, you have to spend the weekend with me—doing whatever I say."

She lifted an eyebrow. "Oh? And if you're wrong?"

"If I'm wrong"—he shrugged—"I have to spend the weekend cooped up here with you, doing whatever *you* say." He grinned. "Either way, I get to spend the weekend with you."

Selena tried to ignore the suggestive glint in his eyes as she pondered the possibilities. Her main task consisted of compiling a final, detailed financial statement in preparation for selling the Aces. She could only imagine Trader's reaction to *that* little plan. On the other hand, she wasn't obliged to tell him her intentions. It was none of his business, after all. She could simply say that the statement was for the stockholders' meeting to be held next week, which was true enough.

"Okay," she said decisively, dropping two large ledgers onto his lap. "If you're so smart, let's see you make something out of these." There was a double motive in her sudden acquiescence. If Trader could really help her with the tedious chore, fine. She wasn't so arrogant that she wouldn't take expert help when it was offered. But if he wasn't serious about streamlining her work, she'd find out fast. The long lists of numbers were enough to bore anyone to death.

Anyone except Trader. As he opened the first book, she half expected him to groan and walk out, but instead he picked up the calculator, spread a clean accounting sheet across the desk with obvious relish, and began working diligently without any encouragement or explanation from her.

"Uh—I haven't told you what I want you to do yet." Her accountants had spent weeks compiling the material in those ledgers. It was up to her to make the final presentation. She eyed him suspiciously. No one, but no one, could possibly decipher those figures so easily. He had to be bluffing.

"I know exactly what you want," he said without slowing his pace. "And I should be done just in time for us to catch the last rays of the sunset in the hills."

She ignored his implication and edged over to his side to watch him for a few more minutes. He was transferring correct cost-accounting figures onto the sheet with dazzling speed and efficiency, and she realized finally that he did indeed know what he was doing.

"Where did you learn how to do that?" she asked, her awe overcoming her former suspicion.

"Hey, I'm a grown-up, remember?" he answered impatiently. "I've learned a thing or two." He glanced up at her, vaguely annoyed. "Don't you have something to do?"

Selena gulped. There was a lot she didn't know about Trader, but this didn't seem like the best time to ask. Marching over to her files, she pulled out a huge folder and began working on the trickiest problem ahead of her—figuring out the net worth of Derringer's largest asset, the Aces.

Right under Trader's nose. She felt a strong twinge of betrayal, but he was the one who had insisted on staying. Perhaps when he saw the final accounting statements of the company he would understand her position better. She looked up at him curiously, wanting to draw him out, but he was happily lost in the sea of numbers, oblivious to her concern.

They worked quietly and companionably for three solid hours before they were interrupted by a phone call. "Selena." Barry's crisp voice broke into the stillness.

Trader hit the button on the intercom without looking up. "What's up?"

"Please tell Selena that NPC Corporation is on the phone again."

Selena's heart practically stopped beating as she held her breath and stared at him. NPC was interested in purchasing the Aces, and her estimates were being drawn up largely for their benefit. She studied Trader's reaction, but he merely said, "Okay," rather absently and went right back to work.

"I—I'll take that call outside," she said into the intercom and, without looking at Trader, hurried into the outer office, carefully closing the door behind her.

"This is Selena Derringer," she said into Barry's phone, casting a nervous glance back at her closed door. "Yes, I'm almost finished now. I'll have the results in the mail to you before five this afternoon. You should get them first thing Monday morning." She looked at her door again, to make sure it was still shut. "Just one more question . . ." she added into the phone. She took a deep breath. "Regarding our latest player, Trader O'Neill. He's been making considerable progress lately. I think you should reconsider dumping him until you've given him a chance . . . No, Mr. Evans, I am not trying to tell you how to run your team, I was merely suggesting—" She gave up and shook her head in defeat. "Very well. I'll have the papers drawn up and delivered right after our stockholders' meeting."

She hung up the phone and sighed. Barry gave her a keen look. "Shall I invent an imaginary meeting for you?" he asked, inclining his head delicately toward her office.

"No, no, Barry," she said. "Thanks anyway. I'll have to face the music myself." She flung the door open and peered inside.

There was Trader, exactly as she had left him, still working away. An unbearable flash of guilt almost threatened to break her—but then she noticed that the receiver button on the intercom was turned off. An alarm instantly went off in her head. Had Trader heard every word of her conversation before turning it off? Or had she been too far away from Barry's intercom for her voice to carry? Trader gave her no clues as she approached.

"How's it going?" she asked him lightly as she picked up her papers.

He looked up at her and smiled, as happy as a boy just finishing his homework. "Just about done," he announced. "And I must say, I'm very impressed. It's amazing how you managed to stay in the black since you bought the Aces. My hat is off to you, Selena," he finished smoothly. "You are an excellent businesswoman."

She was surprised and touched. "Well, thank you," she said sincerely. "I must say, it hasn't been easy." She couldn't resist adding, "It's good to know that you can admit when you're wrong. You thought I was hopelessly unsuited for running a paper-box company, remember?"

The devilish grin returned as if it had never left

his face. "Oh, I haven't changed my mind about that," he announced, coolly looking her up and down. "I still think you're too creative to be satisfied with this. But you did your best, Selena, and that's the important thing."

Back to base one. She swallowed her response as she buzzed for Barry, asking him over the intercom to come in. As he entered a moment later with a batch of correspondence for her to sign, she took the opportunity to slip him her final sales figures on the Aces. "Just put this in an envelope and mail it to Mr. Evans," she said casually, deliberately avoiding Trader's gaze. Barry picked up the cue immediately and slipped out.

"I'm right behind you," Trader announced a moment later. He handed her his figures and smiled. "This should impress the hell out of everyone at the stockholders' meeting."

Selena couldn't believe it. He had transformed the tedious mass of numbers into a logical, consistent order. The endless chore had virtually melted under his expert hand. As she thumbed carefully through the neatly penciled pages, her eyes widened in admiration. The man was truly a wizard. "This is tremendous," she said honestly. "What are you, an accountant?"

"Among other things," he answered evasively. "Also a good gambler. I've won the bet, fair and square. Tell me, do you have a pair of jeans and some rough-and-ready clothes in that closet over there?"

She blinked and nodded reluctantly. "I'm always prepared for anything," she explained. "Why? What did you have in mind?"

He waved her questions away with a careless hand. "Bring some jeans and a warm jacket," he ordered. "It gets pretty cold up there. Meet me at my car outside. You've got exactly five minutes. We can just catch the setting sun."

"It gets cold up *where?*" she demanded, panicking. "I'm not going to let you kidnap me."

"Oh, but you are," he insisted with maddening confidence. "You agreed to this, remember? Surely you don't want to welsh on a bet."

Selena wondered wildly where he meant to take her when the phone rang once more, sounding unusually intrusive. Barry answered it in the outer office, then buzzed Selena over the intercom. "It's your brother, Selena. He just wanted you to know he's going out of town for the weekend. He'll see you on Monday."

"That makes three of us," Trader announced, striding over to the closet. She was too stunned to disagree. She nodded dimly and watched as he selected a pair of jeans, a plaid shirt, a thick sweater, and a sturdy jacket. "Let's get going," he suggested cheerfully. "I promise, you'll be very glad you lost your bet."

"Look, Trader," she said, finding her voice. She sounded to herself like a schoolgirl fending off a merciless debator, but she faced him bravely. "I insist on knowing where you want to take me."

"Why? What difference does it make?" His blue eyes bored into hers, making her distinctly uncomfortable. She knew that look of his by now, and she knew that there wasn't much use in fighting it. His determination would not let up until he had what he wanted. He stalked over to her and took her in his arms. "Don't fight me, honey. The alternative will be so much sweeter." To confirm his brash statement, he bent his head and took her mouth quickly, savoring the warm sensation with obvious enjoyment.

Selena's senses reeled. She clung to him blindly, wanting to lose herself and yet knowing how dangerous this situation was rapidly becoming. "No..." she murmured desperately, her hands pushing weakly against his chest. "I won't be seduced, Trader."

"Why not?" he whispered huskily, sounding suddenly sensible. "Seduction is a very pleasant experience, you know. And I promise to take all the blame if you don't like it." He grinned cheekily, completely confident that she would indeed like it very much. "Admit it, Selena. You've been waiting for this just as much as I have. It's time to find out what we've been missing."

Selena began to panic. The way things were going, they would be lovers before the night ended. She had wanted that with all the longing of her soul, but now there was so much more to it than that. Here she was about to sell the team out from under him, effectively drowning the dream he had cherished for so long. He would hate her when he found out, and he would think her a heartless, ruthless woman who thought nothing of wantonly sharing his bed before plunging in the knife.

But he had also called her an excellent businesswoman, and that she was. Once he considered the sagging numbers, he would have to admit that she had no choice. He would *have* to see it that way, she thought desperately. He'd just have to understand.

Trader let her go and bustled back to the closet,

where he draped his selection of clothes over one arm. "Let's go," he said jauntily.

She took a deep breath and steadied herself. "All right," she said gamely. "But just remember one thing, Trader." She spoke so seriously that he stopped and looked up. "This was your idea. I'll go along with it, but don't forget that you're the one who's insisting."

His eyes twinkled for a moment as if he understood far more than he should. Then his face broke into a satisfied smile. "Fair enough," he said. "You're not responsible." He held out his arm gallantly, waiting to escort her from the room.

She threw back her head, took another deep breath, and marched forward, letting her fingers settle around the hard, unyielding contours of his muscular throwing arm.

It was like magic. Only twenty minutes out of the city, and the concrete and steel were already replaced by the promise of mountains and lush green trees lining both sides of the parkway. Selena let herself relax in the warm but refreshing breeze that permeated Trader's car. She even let herself be reminded that it was just a little bit like northern California. Equally pretty, and in a way, better. Maybe it was just that she hadn't been out of the city for so long. She had been working too hard, and this would be a sorely needed break.

Trader said very little during the drive, seemingly content with his victory. As they traveled north, patches of suburban houses and towns gave way to acres of farmland, until each turn of the road revealed more and more greenery, Victorian farmhouses, and traditional red barns. For over two hours, they drove steadily, exchanging little conversation as their ruffled edges gradually disappeared.

"May I now most humbly ask where we're going?" Selena said as Trader pulled off the highway and headed east onto Route 23.

"East," he answered with a smile.

"I can see that, but where? To your cabin or something?"

"Or something." Trader grinned.

"Another surprise, huh? I hope it's something normal, at least. You have to admit, you don't always do things in a conventional manner. That restaurant you took me to, for example."

"You enjoyed that, didn't you?"

"Well, yes," she admitted. "But only after I got used to it."

One hand left the steering wheel and found hers, giving it a little squeeze. "Trust me."

She stole a sidelong glance at him, hiding her uprush of anticipation. They were driving along amiably enough, but both of them knew that the electricity between them was on the brink of cresting. Selena ordered herself to take it step by step, and for the next hour she watched the alluring scenery pass by. They traveled into western Massachusetts through the town of Great Barrington, and she began to wonder how many states he was planning on traversing. He went farther and farther into Massachusetts, passing through many small villages, until at last she was thoroughly confused. Just when she was about to inquire again as to their destination, Trader suddenly turned down a quiet, one-lane road.

"Route 143," he explained. "We're almost there."

The road was pocketed with one or two houses every mile or so, and Selena caught a glimpse of the sun setting over the mountains whenever there was a break in the lush foliage.

"This is a beautiful area," she breathed quietly.

"We're in the heart of the Berkshires." He continued driving in silence for another fifteen minutes, and the scenery became even more exquisite. White birches lined both sides of the road, providing a natural and elegant border, and Selena couldn't believe it would get any more beautiful, but it did.

"And there's our turnoff," he announced suddenly.

"What turnoff?" She could see nothing except dense greenery on all sides.

A country road appeared magically to the right. Now they were heading at a steep angle down the most exquisite stretch she had ever seen.

"I don't know where we are, and I'm not sure I care," Selena whispered as her ears picked up the sound of constant flowing water. RIVER ROAD, the sign said, and she understood why. The car was paralleling a small meandering river.

"The middle branch of the Westfield River," he explained. "My land is at the bottom of this road in the valley. If you think this is pretty, just wait."

She didn't have to wait long. Trader drove slowly for a few more miles as they passed stately colonial homes on immense plots of cleared land. Mountains protected them on both sides, as if the river had spent the past ten thousand years coursing a path down to the spot where Trader finally pulled off the road.

Selena got out of the car and took a luxurious breath

of cool country air. What she saw was equally breath-taking.

On one side of the road was the river—over twenty feet wide and shooting rapids of bubbling water for thousands of feet, where it disappeared around a narrow bend. Perpendicular to that was a large running brook that fed into the river. Its source was a huge, cascading waterfall that tumbled over the mountain in torrents.

"I've got ten acres," Trader explained as he pointed to the mountains and the surrounding water. "Now," he asked, "is this normal enough for you?"

"No," Selena said teasingly, "but who cares?"

Trader opened the trunk of the car and took out two bags of groceries. "Follow me," he ordered.

"Where did you get that food?" she demanded, growing immediately suspicious.

"I told you, I'm a good gambler."

"You mean you *knew*—"

"I've been waiting all week for this." His smile did nothing to erase her amazement. She followed him up a small incline that led to a clearing next to the brook. When he put the bags of food down and unfolded a blanket, she grew instantly suspicious. "Uh, Trader . . . where's 'your cabin—or something'?"

He looked briefly puzzled, and then laughed. "My cabin? It's not built yet."

- 6 -

SELENA CHOKED. "OH, REALLY? Then what exactly are we doing here?" She frowned in dismay. "I knew it was too good to last." He said nothing, and she stared him down accusingly. "This," she announced, "is definitely not normal."

Trader grinned. "It may or may not be normal. But it *is* beautiful. Come on and help me get all this food out. I'll start a fire and we can watch the sunset."

Selena didn't move. "I am not sleeping out here," she said firmly, "and that's final. I am good at many things, but camping is not one of them. I flunked Girl Scouts, I hate bugs, and anything less than a soft mattress gives me cramps."

Trader continued unpacking, lifting out a roast

chicken, a chocolate cake, several pieces of fruit, and small plastic containers.

"I'm not kidding, Trader. I don't like sleeping bags." He still said nothing, apparently waiting for her to talk herself out. He obviously held all the cards. She couldn't go anywhere without him, and had no choice but to stay with him. He, being the savvy negotiator that he was, realized all this and was simply waiting for her to realize it, too.

"How about a compromise?" she proposed suddenly. His eyes flashed interest, and she was encouraged to continue. "We'll build a fire, and eat here, but then we head to a nice country inn. Agreed?"

"Maybe."

"Maybe? I need an answer, Trader."

He looked at her keenly. "You're too uptight, Selena. For you everything has to be in some inflexible order. What you want is preplanned and prepackaged, but life isn't always like that. You have to roll with the punches."

"I don't need a lesson in spontaneity, if that's what you mean."

"Oh, don't you?"

"No!" she cried. "I like to know what's going on, that's all. And I like to move at my own pace."

"A California snail's pace," Trader commented.

"As opposed to the New Yorker's rat race?"

To her consternation, he laughed and strode off purposefully to gather firewood, muttering something about Victorian values. Selena watched him covertly, the stubbornness in her eyes becoming replaced by feminine awareness. His lean, hard body looked so comfortable trekking through the trees, and he carried himself with masterful ease. He looked for all the world like some god of the forest, ready to bend the woods to his will.

Then it dawned on her. Was he doing all this on purpose, to get back at her for her betrayal? She wasn't about to ask. It was possible that he knew what was going on with the Aces, and yet he had given absolutely no indication that he knew anything more than the latest practice drill. If he was a man about to have a dream shattered, he was either a cockeyed optimist—or he couldn't face the truth. Neither of those descriptions fit Trader O'Neill at all, which meant that he must still be in the dark. She looked over to where Trader was already circling back with his arms full of wood. May as well pitch in, she thought.

Soon they had piled up enough wood for a fire and while Trader set things up, Selena sat by the brook to relax.

"That's my favorite swimming hole," Trader called over to her. He ambled over and pointed to the huge broken dam that diverted the running water, creating a small pond. Walking out on top of the manmade dam that functioned like a bridge, he suddenly began to remove his shirt and shoes. "Last one in is a rotten egg!" he called, breaking into laughter. Without warning, he began to unzip his pants, and Selena found herself suddenly shy, averting her eyes. It wasn't that she had never seen a naked man before, but Trader's decision to skinny-dip was so abrupt that she was completely taken aback.

But she knew that he was challenging her, and this was a perfect opportunity to show him that she could be just as spontaneous as he was.

"Okay, hot shot," she said bravely. "But I think I'll dive in from the other bank." She didn't have to add that the other bank afforded privacy and that she would be able to enter the water unseen.

As she was negotiating her way over the rocks, she heard a sudden splash as Trader jumped in.

"It's glorious," he announced, diving gracefully under the water.

Selena stopped behind a tree and stripped off her outer clothes, debating whether or not to keep on her bra and panties. They provided some cover, but they were, in a way, more provocative than a bathing suit because of their more intimate associations.

"Come on in, already," he called out. "What's taking you so long?"

After a moment's deliberation, she nervously removed her underwear and quickly jumped in. She could hear him swimming around on the other side of the stone-wall dam, and slowly and cautiously made her way along, following the surprisingly swift currents. When at last she was swept around the corner, she saw Trader's head pop up. He grabbed her hand and pulled her out of the currents, taking her into the safety of the swimming hole.

"Isn't this heaven?" he exclaimed, diving under again without warning.

Selena wanted to enjoy the swim, but her thoughts were dominated by the problem of how she was going to get back to her clothes with some dignity. The currents were too strong to fight her way back up and around. Skinny-dipping was one of the things she had flunked in Girl Scouts, she recalled grimly. Her attitude surprised her, but she couldn't help her unexpected modesty. She had been aware of the possibility that she and Trader would have ample opportunity to see each other's bodies when she had agreed to spend the weekend with him, but she hadn't anticipated such a startling introduction.

"Delicious," Trader said as his head popped back up. "After weeks of football practice, it sure beats whirlpool baths in the locker room."

"Do you take them with the other men?" she asked too brightly, and then blanched at the way it had sounded.

"It's a big bathtub," he teased.

She could only imagine guys like Killer Miller and Tank Larson sitting naked in a huge twenty-foot hot tub.

"Of course I prefer different company," he added as he swam over and put his arms around her. His hands began to trace the soft length of her back, and a little shudder of anticipation went through her. Then he stopped cold.

"What's the matter?" she asked nervously. "Is something wrong?"

"And I accused you of not being spontaneous. I take it back." He kissed her gently and continued to stroke her back. Her breasts floated tantalizingly in the water, just out of his sight but not at all out of his reach. His hands grasped her waist and lifted her slightly, so that her lush, rosy-tipped breasts swam invitingly before him. "Lovely," he murmured huskily. "You're as beautiful as I dreamed you would be." Letting her body sink back into the water, he took her breasts in his hands, holding them lightly so that water continued to flow around them.

Selena's blood began to rush and she arched her back slightly so that her breasts were jutting gracefully into his eager hands. He caressed them slowly, with fire and appreciative wonder. Then she felt his hip and her half-lidded eyes flew open in shock.

"You're wearing a bathing suit!" she cried as she ducked lower into the water.

"And you're not."

"That's not fair," she bellowed. "You had it on under your clothes?" He nodded. "I thought we were going to skinny-dip!"

"My mistake," he said with belated gallantry. She glared at him unforgivingly, her eyes practically shooting darts.

"Did you do this on purpose?" she demanded.

"Of course not!" he snapped. "Do you really think I'd trick you into something as ridiculous as this? Really, Selena."

She didn't know what to say next, and Trader watched her confusion grimly. A second later, he squirmed around in the water and produced his bathing trunks, tossing them onto the dry land. "There," he announced. "Is that better?"

She laughed weakly, but stopped when she saw the hunger in his eyes. "Now we're even," she agreed.

He reached out and placed his hands on her bare shoulders, his eyes inviting her to come closer. Suddenly, her inhibitions dropped, and she felt like a free, wanton spirit. Here they were, a man and a woman, together in an exquisite natural setting. The water concealed them and yet offered no protection—an arrangement that somehow suited her at this tentative moment. She edged over to him in the water, her breasts just brushing against the hardness of his chest.

She heard him give a sharp little intake of breath before his hands dropped to mold the feminine contours of her waist. Then he guided her closer to the shore so that their bare feet found the silty floor of the pond and they were able to stand free.

Selena was trembling with anticipation, and Trader did not disappoint her. He drew her slowly into his arms, clearly relishing the silken electricity that claimed them when their bodies touched, and kissed her with a passionate deliberation that left her senses reeling. The kiss lasted for a priceless eternity, spinning them both into a vortex that existed only for them. But then Trader surprised her.

He drew back slightly, his arms still holding her close, and whispered, "Not yet, sweet. Not now, not like this."

Selena blinked in aroused confusion, unwilling to shamelessly urge him. "What—what's wrong?" she asked.

"Nothing. Everything is perfect." His hands slid down her back. "But it's getting dark, and it gets very cold up here at night." His eyes softened intimately. "Come on. Let's let the fire warm us up for now. We can warm ourselves up later." She smiled shyly, and he gallantly swam with her back to the other shore, where she climbed over the rocks to retrieve her clothes.

The sun was just behind the mountains, turning the sky a deep red as Selena and Trader sat in front of the campfire. Selena breathed the country air in deeply, letting it soothe her. She stretched and looked up just in time to see a large cloud sweeping across the sky, blocking out the tiny light of the first evening star. In front of her, the fire crackled invitingly, and the brook added its bubbling music as the trees whispered in the cool breeze.

Trader had taken care of everything. They sat on a large blanket that he had set like a dinner table. There were bright red picnic plates, real silverware, wineglasses, and red and white striped linen napkins. The roast chicken had been expertly carved, and cold string beans and buttermilk rolls had been arranged in their own serving dishes. Selena was biting hungrily into a roll as Trader lifted an ear of corn wrapped in tin foil from the fire. Opening it carefully, he smiled as the steamy aroma was released.

"I wouldn't have flunked Girl Scouts if you had been around to tutor me," she said as they began to eat. "You have hidden talents, Trader. Tell me, do you also do windows?"

He broke the corn in half and handed her a piece. "As a matter of fact, yes. I once had a roommate who taught me everything there is to know about domestic life. You name it, and I do it—clean, cook, iron shirts. I can even bake homemade bread."

"I'm impressed," Selena said as she munched on the corn. "My former roommates were bona fide slobs. I guess men are really better qualified to keep house," she teased.

"My roommate in question wasn't a man," he informed her.

"Oh." There was a sudden silence. "I thought you meant—"

"Five years in a one-bedroom apartment in New York." Trader spoke casually, but Selena was taken aback. She wanted to know when and why this liaison had ended, but didn't have the nerve to ask.

"It ended by simply running out of gas," he filled in. "Just sputtered out. Neither one of us wanted to go for a refill."

"Five years is a long time," she observed quietly. "Were you . . ."

"Married?" He shook his head. "Oh, no, it was strictly live-in, with no commitments." He shrugged gamely, but his face betrayed a lingering sadness.

"Do you still think about . . . her?" Selena asked hesitantly.

He blinked in surprise. "What? No, of course not."

"You looked so sad there for a moment."

He smiled ruefully. "You're perceptive. No, there was no love lost by the time we broke up. None at all."

She didn't want to pry, but he seemed to want to talk about it. "What happened?" she pressed gently.

Trader sighed. "Oh, I don't know. And that's just the problem. When it came right down to it, I just couldn't make the final commitment. Everything was there—we were a good match, we had a pleasant enough life—but the thought of legally binding my-self to her for the rest of my life . . ." He sighed again, heavily. "I just couldn't face it. And then, everything just fell apart." He shook his head and turned back to his meal, tossing a stick into the fire.

"Maybe she just wasn't the right one," Selena sug-gested softly.

"Obviously not." He evidently thought his tone had been too sharp, and he reached over and took her hand in a silent apology. "It's just that I always wondered if there was something wrong with *me*. If I would react that way in any relationship, balking at the last minute."

Selena said nothing. She wasn't about to give him a knee-jerk reassurance. *Would* he shy away from a commitment with anyone else? With her? She stole a glance at him, wondering feverishly if she were in for a fall. Trader's fingers tightened convulsively around hers for a moment, and her heart opened to him. "I— I don't know," she said at last, giving him the absolute truth. "But . . . I guess . . . we'll find out." She hoped she hadn't said too much, but then Trader smiled.

"Come on, Selena," he said. "Haven't you ever had doubts about a lifetime commitment?"

"In a way," she answered slowly. "But it was a different kind of relationship."

Trader feigned shock. "You mean I'm not the first man you've ever been involved with?"

"Very funny." She threw a little pebble at him before continuing. "Todd was Henry's college roommate."

"At Michigan?"

"Yes. As a matter of fact, it was a year after *you* graduated."

"Oh, I see. Well, you were just a babe in the woods, no doubt."

Selena smiled knowingly. "Maybe," she hedged. "But I was old enough to be engaged."

His face changed. "That's serious. What happened?"

"Dad died. The marriage was postponed while Henry and I shouldered the task of maintaining the company." Selena frowned, remembering the lean years. "All the business degrees in the world couldn't have taught me what I learned in my first year."

"Experience is a wonderful teacher."

"In this case, we almost drove a successful company into the ground. We were children in a world of high competition. Our competitors knew it and took advantage of us."

"But you beat them, and how. I remember now." Trader looked up, gathering his thoughts. "In 1979, your stock plunged twenty-seven points in a year."

"That's right." Selena was amazed at the precision of his recollection. "How did you know that?"

Trader ignored her question. "Then you recovered somehow."

"I landed that huge cereal account," Selena noted with justifiable pride. "We reorganized our sales force and crawled back up. In three years, we topped the market at forty-two and a quarter. We've been stable ever since."

"So what happened to your fiancé?"

"We didn't make it. Henry tried to bring him into the business, but he just couldn't hack it. The fact that I could really bugged him. Besides, he couldn't handle the competition that sprang up between us. After all, I was his boss in a way. I guess that was his biggest hangup. His ego got in the way of our relationship." She looked at Trader shrewdly and added one final note. "You know, Trader, I'm your boss, too, in a way."

"Are you?" he asked coolly. He was watching her, his blue eyes flickering in the firelight. The shadow of a smile lit his features, giving him a slightly mysterious look, and a little chill ran through her when she caught the glimmer of desire in his eyes. She looked back at the fire, pretending not to notice, but his hand reached over and found hers, closing around it gently.

The invisible fire that had been kindling between them for so long jumped suddenly into flame, fanned by the intimacy that was quietly growing in this peaceful setting. Trader lifted Selena's hand and turned it over, tenderly placing warm, tantalizing kisses on the sensitive palm and then kissing each individual fingertip. Selena caught her breath, watching his face in fascination. A shock of dark hair had fallen over his forehead, and the passion that was etched in his features was thrilling to behold. It was plain that he wanted her deeply, and that knowledge added to her own desire.

"Come here," he whispered raggedly. "I want you so much, Selena."

She tumbled against him, her face lifting for the kiss she knew would come. He lowered his mouth to hers without preamble, tasting her sweetness delicately before his tongue found the silky depths inside. Their hands searched and found each other, his resting provocatively just above her breasts, and hers twining gracefully around his neck.

The kiss was long and dreamy, spinning them into a whirlwind that was alive with heightened sensuality. She was trembling, and wanted nothing more than to finish what they had begun.

She saw his eyes soften, but his jaw settled into a tight mold. "Trust me, Selena," he said persuasively. "Tonight, let me be the boss."

She couldn't say no. Her eyes shone her assent, but she whispered earnestly, "Shouldn't we find a place to spend the night?"

"What's wrong with right here?" His hands moved lightly up and down her arms. "Just relax, and I'll show you how beautiful the outdoors can really be."

Selena resisted his seductive words and squinted at him in the firelight. "You like to get your own way, don't you?" She hated to break the mood, but something goaded her to insist. Trader didn't answer, but his hands continued their arousing journey over her arms, and his eyes danced with quiet amusement. Selena could see that he still fully expected her to give in. "You don't know how to compromise, Trader, do you?" she persisted.

He blinked, and his hands abruptly stilled. "Maybe not," he said, "but I do know that it will be glorious if we spend the night here."

"We won't be spending the night here."

She remained firm, and he took her hands in both of his, riveting her with the irresistible blue-eyed gaze she had come to know so well.

"We're not staying," she continued. "We're not."

He kissed her again, sending tiny darts of fire through her blood. Before she could stop him, his hands were teasing the sensitive peaks of her breasts and his mouth dipped to find the hollow of her throat and the tender side of her neck. Her eyes closed unwillingly when his hands found their way inside her shirt, arousing her breasts into a new fullness.

"No, Trader . . ." she moaned, but it was too late. With a cry of surrender, she fell back on the blanket and let him open her shirt, reveling in the lushness of her breasts as he took them in his mouth one by one.

He continued to stroke them with his hands as he raised his head and looked up at her. "You are exquisite, Selena," he said huskily. "You're cool and correct on the outside, but the fire inside you is only waiting to be started." His hands continued their sweet torment, never stopping as he murmured, "Let me love you, sweetheart. I want to know all of you, to be as close to you as I can." She couldn't believe the intensity of her own desire, all from his one entrancing caress. There was nothing she could do but nod weakly and hold out her arms to take him in.

Their clothes seemed to fall away while he explored and delighted in every inch of her soft body. The very earth seemed to welcome them as the night breezes rustled and closed in around them, lifting them out of the real world.

Trader repeated her name over and over, before and after kissing her shoulders, her breasts, her stomach, and the tender insides of her thighs. Selena sat up and shook the hair from her eyes, her breathing ragged as she looped her arms around his neck and kissed him with sensual abandon. Her hands discovered the hard, unyielding planes of his body, which squirmed beneath her butterfly touch, and she delighted in the feminine power that rendered him helpless as she explored his strength.

With a passionate cry, Trader sat up with her and lifted her so that her legs opened to straddle his. His manhood thrust against her silky wetness, caressing it and drawing forth a fountain of response.

"Now, Trader," she pleaded, throwing her head back and pressing her body against his. "I need you."

They joined together swiftly, each shuddering with grateful ecstasy as the pleasure enveloped them. Selena clung to him and rose and fell with him, every cell in her body alive and tingling with excitement. She punctuated each thrust with a little cry of passion, her legs encircling his body to hold him as deeply inside of her as she could.

Trader leaned his head back and studied her ardent face with awe. "You're a bonfire for me, Selena," he whispered raggedly, his eyes closing and unclosing as she tightened her body around him. "I've never seen such passion."

She tried to shake her head, to tell him that it wasn't her, but she could only cry, "For you, Trader! Only for you."

He crushed her against him and led her into a timeless dream that exploded with crashing, swirling colors. They ceased to be two people and became a single being, united on a level that transcended the elemental forces commanding them.

When they had reached the pinnacle and cried out their release, Selena became dimly aware of the tears that had escaped her eyes and fallen into her hair as she leaned against him. She was spent and drowsy, brimming with budding love and gratitude for the magic they had created.

Trader pulled the edge of the blanket over them and kissed her forehead. "I'd better get the sleeping bags from the car," he murmured.

She smiled gently at him and cupped his face in her hands. "We're not sleeping here," she said mockingly.

He kissed her again. "I'm the boss, remember?"

"Not anymore." Her fingers played with his hair. "That was for a limited time only."

"Oh, I see. Well, I have the car keys, remember?"

She put her hand to his lips to stifle him. "It doesn't

matter. There's a force greater than you or me."

He kissed her hand. "What's that?"

"I'm referring to Mother Nature." She looked up at the starless sky filled with clouds. "They've been gathering for over an hour now. I don't think we have much more time before we get it."

Suddenly, a streak of lightning lit up the sky.

"Let me rephrase that. I think we're about to get it, and good."

In the next instant, the clouds unleased a torrent, the rain gathering force swiftly and mercilessly as the night blackened around them.

"Quick!" he shouted. "Gather everything up!"

Blanket, plates, cups, forks, knives, and pieces of fruit were all thrown together pell-mell as they made a mad dash for the car. By the time they got there, totally drenched and out of breath, they were gasping and hooting with laughter. Trader jammed his key into the lock and opened the door for Selena. She dived inside, shaking the water from her short hair as she dumped everything haphazardly into the back seat. Trader joined her a moment later, plunging headfirst into the small car so that he landed practically in her lap.

This brought another burst of laughter that lasted a full five minutes.

"Well, you were right," he admitted. "We're not sleeping outside." He turned on the ignition, and a moment later they were heading up the road. Selena leaned her head against his shoulder, thinking that this moment was absolutely perfect.

But the perfection was short-lived. As she settled down and recovered from the sensual feast she had just experienced, she remembered with a jolt what she had been concealing from Trader. Suddenly, she knew that she could keep it a secret no longer, not after the intimacy they had shared. Her heart swelled. Nothing mattered now except her need to be close to him, without the barrier of secrecy between them.

"Trader," she said softly, searching for the right words. "I have something to tell you."

He squeezed her hand as he maneuvered the car around a bend in the road, the rain pelting against the windshield. "What?"

She decided to just say it, straight out. "I—I hope you won't think this is a bad time to tell you, but— I've decided I have to sell the team." Her words fell into the silence like sticks of dynamite, but Trader's firm profile didn't budge.

"You want to run that by me again?" he asked calmly. Too calmly, Selena thought.

"I can't hide it from you anymore," she said urgently. "I *have* to do it, Trader. I've been planning it for weeks."

Something jumped in the immovable profile, and he grimaced. "I don't believe this. I don't believe *you.*"

A stab of guilt shot through her. "You heard my conversation this afternoon, didn't you?"

"What conversation?"

"With NPC." She tried to explain. "They were one of the original bidders for the Aces back when we first met in February. They still want the team and—" She looked at him feebly. "I can't believe you didn't hear my conversation with them this afternoon."

"Well, believe it," he said sharply. "I did not eaves-drop, if that's what you mean. I'm not a spy, Selena." His words pierced her like knives.

"You can't be angry with me," she pleaded. "I know how much the team means to you, but I am responsible for my company, and the Aces were just a poor investment."

The dam broke. Without warning, Trader swerved to the side of the road, the tires screeching against the wet asphalt. The car stopped with a rude bump, throw-ing them both forward. "Not true," he fired back, his voice as cold as steel. "It's an excellent investment. Only it's an investment you can't understand." His hands tightened on the steering wheel. "Like you can't understand a lot of things."

Selena's heart sank as she struggled to defend her-self. "So you think I'm just a heartless user?"

He didn't answer her at first. The rain was beating monotonously against the roof of the car, and she could almost hear him thinking. "I was hoping," he began softly, "that I could bring out in you things that have been dormant for years. I see a woman who works in extremes. Everything is either black or white. You say I don't compromise, but neither do you."

"Is that why you brought me up here?" she asked. "To seduce me into not selling the Aces?"

"You can't sell the Aces," he said flatly. His eyes glinted blue steel. "Only the chairman of the board of Derringer can do that. And you are not the chairman of the board, remember?"

"Not yet," she said, wanting to bite her tongue the moment she said it.

But Trader didn't challenge her leading remark. He

threw her a warning glance that made her blood curl,
then swung the car back onto the road, his expression
rigid and unyielding. "Not ever," he whispered, sending a chill through her that had nothing to do with the
rain.

- 7 -

SELENA WOKE THE next morning to find herself quite alone. With unerring intuition, she knew at once that everything had changed, and her heart sank.

The previous night had been laced with tension after her revelation about selling the team, and now, even in the half-clutches of sleep, she wished she had kept her company secrets to herself. The first stirrings of love had opened more than her heart. Now she had betrayed both her company and her heart. She had no idea where Trader was, and to make matters worse, the chilly rain was still pattering noisily against the window as if to herald impending doom.

They had driven for close to an hour through the storm until they had come upon this quaint country inn. It should have been supremely romantic; how-

ever, it was anything but. Exhausted and anxious by
the time they arrived, all they could do was fall into
bed and go to sleep. Selena wanted desperately to
crawl into Trader's arms and stay there, but he had
kept pointedly to his side of the bed.

Why had she been so stupid as to tell him about
the deals she was arranging? she wondered anxiously
as she sat up and rubbed her eyes. He now knew
everything there was to know about her, but she realized with a jolt of dismay that she still knew next
to nothing about him—except that he had changed
her life and had stimulated the most intense feelings
she had ever had for any man.

Dressing quickly, she left the flower-papered room
and headed down the long hallway to the main lobby,
where she spied Trader talking animatedly on a pay
phone. She waved tentatively, and when he saw her,
he immediately hung up.

"What's wrong with the phone in our room?" she
asked, and immediately wanted to bite her tongue.
She was only contributing to the less-than-romantic
mood she knew she would encounter.

"I didn't want to wake you." He spoke easily, but
she wasn't fooled. There was clearly much more to
it than that, and she had the distinct feeling that she
wasn't going to find out what it was. He gave her a
cool smile and suggested breakfast. There was nothing
to do but agree.

The dining room was charming, with lace curtains
at the Colonial-style windows and pale blue and lav-
ender wallpaper. They sat down silently, and Trader
announced, "We'll be driving back to New York right
after breakfast."

His words had the effect of a bomb dropping, immediately confirming her worst suspicion. Selena stared at him in amazement. "But—but I thought we were here for the weekend!" she sputtered.

"The weekend?" he repeated, with just the slightest hint of sardonic irony. "Forget it. I have to get back to my office by this afternoon." He spoke with such finality that she knew she didn't have a prayer. She also knew she was witnessing a chilling side of him that she wasn't sure she even wanted to see again, and for a moment she was almost afraid of him.

"Office?" she echoed lamely, feeling more and more alienated. It was the first time he had ever mentioned a real place of business to her, and suddenly it sounded unreasonably menacing.

"Yes, my office." He spoke as if he had been going to his office every day, and for a moment Selena wondered if he had. Trader was rapidly turning into a stranger before her eyes, and she wanted to cry and rage at him at the same time. "Sorry," he said, "but I've got football practice straight through the week. Today's the only time I can take care of business, so the vacation is canceled."

She stared at him in disbelief. "What—what business do you have?"

He didn't answer her. Instead, he consulted the menu and ordered a hearty repast of French toast, orange juice, bacon, blueberry muffins, and coffee. Suddenly without appetite, Selena chose orange juice and coffee. They discussed the possibility of the rain letting up in overly polite tones until the waitress brought their orders. Then the tension became too much to bear.

"What's happening between us?" Selena asked bluntly.

"Quite a lot," Trader answered. "Last night you ruined a perfectly good evening by your revelation that you were intending to sell the Aces."

"And I also told you that I don't feel great about it, but it's a financial necessity. And that I hoped you would understand." Her eyes beseeched him, but he didn't answer, and her temper rose for the first time. Couldn't he see that she was only trying to do her job? To take care of the business without letting personal feelings get in the way? She added baitingly, "Football really is the only thing on your mind, isn't it?"

"The only thing on my mind right now is stopping you from hurting me." His voice was flinty and devoid of emotion. The effect was unnervingly powerful, as if a volcano were ready to erupt just beneath his cool surface.

"Look, Selena," he said. "Ever since you came into my life it's been one obstacle after another. First you outbid me for the Aces; then, after helping me get on the team, you turn around and decide to sell me out. You think nothing of spending the night in my arms and then stabbing me in the back. What kind of woman are you, anyway? I can't wait to see what other little surprises you have in store for me."

"How can you turn on me like this?" she cried, deeply stung. "Besides," she went on, groping for some way to reach him, "even if I sold the team, what makes you think you won't still be able to play?"

"I am going to continue playing," he said stonily as he downed the last of his coffee. "Only now I am going to have to fight you to do it."

"What's that supposed to mean?"

"It means," he said as his cup rattled into the saucer, "that you are about to learn who you are really dealing with."

"Who?" she cried. "Don't you think it's about time you ended the mystery? Especially after last night?"

Trader lifted an eyebrow. *"Especially* after last night," he agreed dryly.

"Just what are you talking about?"

He smiled coldly. "Let's just say that you're about to find out why they call me Trader."

Selena gestured impatiently, but her hand was trembling. "What am I going to learn from some old college nickname?"

"I didn't get it in college," he said pointedly. "It's a name I earned on Wall Street." He rose from his chair and threw down his napkin. "Starting right now, you and I are playing on opposite teams. Only I have the advantage. Do you know why?"

Her heartbeat quickened with a sudden stab of fear. "No, why?"

"Because I've got the ball. And therefore we play by my rules now."

"You've got it all figured out, haven't you?"

He didn't flinch. "Yes."

"How can you be so cold-hearted?" she cried, tears springing to her eyes. She blinked them back.

"I believe you're the cold-hearted one," he replied as he glanced at his watch.

The small gesture inflamed her. He was so busy worrying about the time that he wasn't even thinking about her. Suddenly, everything that had looked so

promising had turned into a total disaster. Selena swallowed hard and stood up.

"Then I guess there's nothing more to say."

"At last we agree," he retorted, signaling for the
check.

Fifteen minutes later, they were in the car, on their
way back to New York. Neither of them said a word.

In the days that followed, Selena never heard from
Trader at all. It was as if he had vanished into thin
air. She finally broke down and called Eli to see if
Trader had made practice, and became even more
alarmed when she learned that he hadn't shown up
even once. When Eli and Henry tried calling him,
they were met with an answering machine, and Henry
grew afraid that something had happened to the Ace's
quarterback.

But there was enough activity at the office to keep
her occupied. As the stockholders' meeting came closer
and closer, there was a sudden upsurge of trading in
Derringer stock. Overnight, Derringer seemed to have
acquired a new status, becoming of new and immediate interest to every broker in town. The excitement
helped to boost the stock prices higher and higher,
until by Wednesday morning, Derringer Industries was
the talk of Wall Street.

Selena was sure that it had to do with the rumors
that were circulating about her selling the Aces for a
considerable sum. The sizable profit had bolstered a
frenzy of trading, and there was no end in sight. The
recent development cast a new light on the state of
the company, and this, combined with the internal
changes that had shaped her life recently, brought her

to some new and unexpected decisions.

Of course, Henry, still in the dark about her plans to sell the Aces, had another theory as to why there was so much excitement in the stock market.

"It's incredible, Selena." Henry stood holding the front page of *The Wall Street Journal* only inches from his sister's face as he hooted aloud at the headlines. "'Derringer stocks continue to see heavy trading,'" he began reading.

While he beamed with excitement, Selena looked out the window of the stadium office, down to where the Aces were practicing. There was still no sign of number eleven.

"I already read it, Henry," she said absently.

"So what do you think of the Aces now?" he asked proudly.

She turned slowly and looked at him. "What?"

"The Aces, the Aces!" he raved. "Why do you think our stock has soared seven points in the past few days? It *has* to be—my spending all that money to purchase the best players in the league has paid off."

"But at what cost?" Selena reminded him. "Remember, Henry, you sold close to thirty percent of your interest in Derringer."

Henry laughed at her. "With the stock going sky-high, my remaining shares are now worth enough to recoup all the money I spent."

Selena knew she had to stop misleading him. She had made a devastating mistake with Trader. She wasn't about to repeat it. "Henry," she said softly, "I have a confession to make."

Her brother was still bursting with energy, but when

he saw the stricken look on her face, he sat down and looked at her expectantly. "What now, Selena? We've been through enough together to make any new crisis just another problem. It can't be that bad."

Selena sat down opposite her brother and explained all the moves she had been secretly planning, leaving nothing out. His eyes widened with shock when she came to the part about selling the Aces, but he let her continue. When she told him of her strategy to vote herself in as chairman of the board, he gave her an odd little smile.

"Do you want to be chairman of the board, Selena?"

"No," she admitted. "I did, but—" She sank lower in her seat and threw up her arms in complete surrender. "For the first time in my life, I don't know what I want. I only know what I *don't* want. And I do not want to continue running Derringer Industries."

There was a long pause. "What about selling the Aces?" Henry asked finally.

"That's just it, Henry. I was planning on selling, but now...I—I've changed my mind." Her voice trembled slightly, but she beamed with the relief of her decision. Henry was regarding her with complete astonishment. "It's incredible what you've done with that team. You do know football, Henry. But as for me...there has to be more to life than paper boxes. I'm bored. I want to liven up my dull cardboard life." She sat up and faced him bravely. "Next week at the stockholders' meeting, I'm going to announce my resignation. I'm also going to squelch any rumors about selling the Aces. From now on it's our football team and no one else's."

Henry fell back in his seat and rubbed his head.

"Whew! When did you have this sudden change of heart?"

"I've had a lot of time to think about it," she said slowly. "You can thank Trader for that. Somehow he's had a big effect on my thinking. And dreaming," she added. "I guess I just needed someone to come along and"—she threw up her arms—"help me tackle the problem."

"Terrific!" Henry said. "Only now I have a problem." He pointed down at the field. "I'm still out a quarterback."

"Leave that to me," Selena said with a mysterious little smile. "That's one job I think I can handle."

She walked out, feeling lighter and freer than she had since the move to New York. Even the stadium felt different now, almost friendly and warm instead of a terrible burden. Now all she had to do was find Trader—and she knew just the place to look.

"Five shots of tequila, please."

It was Trader's voice, and she whipped around from the bar to see him leaning against a stool. He was dressed impeccably in a suit, much like the first time she had seen him here.

"Trader?" She did her best to cover her surprise, and her relief at seeing him. "You surprised me."

"I'm full of surprises." He grinned devilishly, held up a copy of *The Wall Street Journal*, and tossed it on the bar.

She reread the headlines and laughed. "All the rumors about selling the Aces really drove up the stock, didn't they?" she began, but Trader broke in impatiently.

"Is that what you think? That the price has gone up because of the rumors?" He shook his head as if faced with a very dim-witted person. "You're just as blind as ever, aren't you?"

"Blind?" She shook her head and waved her hands in dismissal, eager to explain. "No, no, you don't understand. I'm—"

"Oh, I understand, more than you think. You see, my dear Ms. Chairman, your stocks aren't soaring because of any rumors. It's actually much simpler than that." He leaned an elbow against the bar and let his magnetic blue eyes capture hers. "Let me be the first to inform you. You're about to face what is known as a proxy fight."

Selena froze. It took another second for her thoughts to unscramble. "A proxy fight." She was utterly stunned. "Are you telling me someone is trying to take controlling interest of my company?"

The bartender brought over a bottle of tequila and a shot glass, and Trader held up five fingers. "Four more glasses," he ordered. "One for each shot." After the bartender complied, Trader picked up the bottle and slowly and meticulously began filling each shot glass to the top. "The trouble with you, my dear Ms. Derringer, is that you're too uptight. You need to relax."

"Is that why you took me up to the Berkshires, to relax me?" she choked out.

He finished pouring the last drink and put the bottle down. "I took you to the Berkshires because I wanted to share something with you." He spoke smoothly, but there was the same underlying anger that had devastated her before. "But you had other plans in mind. That's when I realized what a fool I had been. There I was, helping you with your business. And all along you were planning to turn my help into profits for yourself, leaving me out in the cold."

"That's not true," Selena tried to protest, but it was futile and she knew it. He would have no reason to believe her now. "So what are your plans?" she asked dully. "Are you going to go back to practice tomorrow, or are you orchestrating this proxy fight?"

"Both," he said coolly. "But this proxy fight is more than my personal revenge. I'm going to safeguard my future, protect what I've built up."

She stared at him incredulously. He was dead serious, and he had admitted that he was somehow involved in this proxy fight for Derringer Industries.

"What's your role in all this?" she demanded.

"My role? You mean, how am I involved in taking control of your company?" He smiled with mock innocence. "I'm not a corporate climber, Selena." It was the first time he had spoken her name, and the sound of it sent a curious chill through her. "I'm just a stockbroker."

"A stockbroker who sells enough shares in my company to let the buyers have control of it," she said angrily. "You'd better drink those tequilas, Trader. The fight isn't over yet."

The cool smile remained on his face. "Oh, these aren't for me," he explained dryly, picking up the first glass. "They're for you. You're going to need them."

She took the glass from his hand and stared into its depths. She wanted to throw it in his face, but she couldn't move, couldn't do anything except stand there. Tears of rage and betrayal sprang to her eyes, and she did nothing to dispel them. Her hand trembled violently, and she let the glass clatter back onto the bar, its contents spilling over her hand. Without looking at Trader, she turned and fled.

Fired by the confused anger and pain, Selena walked the city streets for hours without knowing where she was going. She tried desperately to regain some insight and balance, but all she could think about was revenge. Trader had come into her life and turned everything upside down. First he had challenged her, then he had rejected her, and now he had declared all-out war. The worst of it was that even though one part of her wanted to strangle him, another, deeper part of her still wanted to love him. The power and sense of control he radiated both frightened and attracted her. And she yearned for his iron will to bend itself in her direction.

Selena did not know until the day of the stockholders' meeting exactly what the final tabulation would be in the proxy fight that Trader was pursuing. The question was whether or not he could amass enough shares to allow his buyers a controlling interest. The day before the meeting, the Derringers—Selena and Henry between them—still had enough shares to maintain control, but that was no guarantee, even at that late date. Selena wondered nervously how Trader would react if he lost. Not that it mattered, she thought bitterly. There didn't seem to be much chance of a reconciliation between them either way.

She walked into the stockholders' meeting a little late the next day, allowing Henry the chance to explain that she would be leaving the company. By now the

news of the proxy fight had received national attention, and it still remained to be seen who would have
control.

Selena had dressed in a sober business suit for the
meeting. She had stayed awake half the night, going
over and over all the figures she would be presenting.
But when she entered the room, it was clear that she
would not be making any presentations at all.

Standing at the front of the room addressing over
fifty people was Trader O'Neill. When he saw her, a
delighted smile lit up his face.

"Well, good morning," he said heartily. "Nice of
you to join us. We reserved a seat for you right up
front." He gestured to an empty seat next to Henry,
but Selena remained frozen where she was.

"Is this some kind of a joke?" she asked.

"Joke?" Trader arched a brow. "Hardly. I've just
been going over our annual report." He flipped through
the pages of the report Selena had put together for the
meeting and nodded his head in approval. "Very im-
pressive," he said. "This company was well worth
fighting for."

A few of the men in the front row revealed triumphant smiles, and Selena knew at once that they were
there because of Trader. She marched over and took
a seat next to Henry, totally and uneasily surrounded
by new faces.

"Where are all our people?" Selena whispered to
Henry.

"Your people sold out to us," Trader answered her.
"And the new stockholders have seen fit to elect me
chairman of the board." He pretended to ignore the
shock that raged across her face as he continued

smoothly, "It's not official yet, of course, but I have the control base to make it happen. Now, if you don't mind, we have an enormous amount of work to cover at this meeting and very little time."

"You!" she sputtered. *"You're* the new chairman? This is ridiculous." She stood up and approached him. "It wasn't enough that you destroyed our interest? You had to *personally* take over the company?" The fury that propelled her chastened everyone in the room except Trader. He met her fiery gaze head-on, his countenance deliberately cool. She was harboring more than fury, of course, but only Trader knew that and only he could see it. The stinging hurt, the knowledge that he had used her in the most personal way, was slicing through her like a knife.

"It seemed much more efficient this way," he explained. Helpless to contradict him, she turned and looked at Henry for confirmation, while the people in the room remained politely, ominously, quiet.

"He's the boss now," Henry said solemnly. "He's carrying the ball. So we play by his rules."

Trader beamed. "Which brings me to my first announcement and primary decision as the new chairman of the board." He looked around the room for a moment, pausing dramatically. "The Aces are not for sale, at any price. Derringer Industries is keeping the team, and from now on it will be the major asset and focus for future growth."

Selena seemed to be the only one in the room who was surprised by this revelation. Trader continued, oblivious to the look on her face. "And just so there are no hard feelings, Henry, I'm designating you as president of the Aces. You've done an excellent job so far, and I see no reason to change that."

Henry blinked and then smiled tentatively, as the information sank in. Selena realized that he would now be perfectly happy, as long as he had his beloved team. She was virtually on her own.

"I see several ways to increase the income from "The Aces in the immediate future," Trader went on. "The first is to start a cheerleading squad—something along the order of the Dallas Cowboys cheerleaders."

"Hah!" Selena said scornfully. "A bunch of scantily clad girls prancing around on the field? That's a ridiculous idea!"

"It is not ridiculous," Trader countered calmly. "The Cowboys show a marked increase in attendance because of their cheerleaders, and we could easily do the same. In fact," he added, addressing her directly, "I was thinking this might be an area you'd want to take charge of."

"Me?" She almost choked. "Are you serious?"

"Sure," he said easily, without a trace of humor. "I thought you could use something lighter, a little more fun than paper boxes."

"Absolutely not!" she shouted. "I will not—"

"We'll discuss it later. I'd like to continue uninterrupted," Trader said politely, but the command in his voice was unmistakable. He gestured for her to sit down, and after a moment she did. She needed time to gather her composure and think clearly.

For the next hour, Selena was forced to listen as Trader explained the ways in which he was going to totally rework the company. What had been a pleasantly profitable business was now being pushed to the extreme. Trader was a risk taker. He was going to raise as much capital as he could to expand Derringer's role in sports. The Aces were only the beginning. Within two years, he was shooting for a baseball team, and possibly a soccer team.

"So much for cardboard boxes," Selena said after the meeting broke up. "By next week, our assets will be measured by our standings in the NFL rather than the stock exchange."

Everyone filed out, and she watched as Trader shook hands and deftly handled the good-byes to people who were obviously his clients. His confidence and aura of command assured them that their investments were in good hands.

Henry put his hand on Selena's arm to guide her away, but she wasn't going anywhere until she had faced Trader O'Neill. Maybe it was too late to save her company, but there might be something left of her pride to salvage.

- 8 -

"TERRIFIC," SELENA MUTTERED sarcastically as she dumped the contents of her desk into a Derringer corrugated box. "I hope his clients understand that he hoodwinked them into buying a failing company."

Henry sat on the opposite side playing with a paperweight. "You don't hoodwink investors of that magnitude," he said. "They know what they're getting for their money."

"Of course they do!" Trader's voice was not the one Selena wanted to hear at that moment, but there he was, leaning against the doorway with his arms folded, watching her intently. "They get season's tickets to all the games," he added with a triumphant chuckle. "That's the reason they bought in. They just want to own part of a football team."

"Then they're as crazy as you and Henry!" Selena exploded bitterly. "You're all nuts. A bunch of grown men with a lot of money, acting like kids."

"Maybe," Trader conceded. "But this is one kid who couldn't afford to have his dreams broken by you."

"You are so blind, Trader," she said, shaking her head with grim finality. She closed her eyes for a moment. "You think you've orchestrated a miracle, and it wasn't even necessary. It so happens that as of last week, I changed my mind about selling the Aces."

Trader stopped, clearly unwilling to believe her. She could see it in the flinty set of his eyes. But Henry intervened.

"That's true, Trader," he interjected. "You don't know it, but you went through this proxy fight all for nothing."

Trader was still skeptical. "You expect me to believe that?"

"Believe what you want," Henry said. "I'm telling you the truth. Selena came to me last week and explained everything—concluding with her decision *not* to sell. She said she wanted to go into something new, that she needed a change." Selena listened dully as her words and revelations, which had seemed so bright and full of promise at the time, were repeated earnestly by her brother. They didn't seem to matter now. She had opened her heart to Trader, and he had betrayed her. It was too late. "She said it had to do with something you two had been talking about," Henry finished quietly.

Something in Trader's granite countenance seemed

to flicker. He turned to her with a glimmer of hope in his eyes. "Is this true, Selena?"

She stared at him darkly, refusing to answer.

"Is that what you wanted to tell me in the bar?" he asked, comprehension dawning. He waited again for an answer from her, but she remained deadly silent.

"Come on now, speak up," he said, taking a stab at joviality. "That's an order. After all, I'm your boss now."

"You were *almost* my boss," she corrected him coldly. "I quit, remember?" She put the box on her desk, and dumped the entire contents of the top drawer into it in one swoop. "I'm leaving, as of right now."

Henry looked at Trader and shrugged. "She means it, Trader. Selena has had it as the CEO of Derringer. I've been thinking about how to replace her all week."

Trader's face began to change quickly, and all at once Selena's heart began beating again. She could see exactly what was going to happen. She was in the driver's seat again, and Trader was about to find that out—the hard way. A spark of hope stole back into her eyes, and glancing at her brother she realized Henry saw it, too.

"Yes," Trader said, nodding. He approached her desk trying to think of what to say next. "But surely—"

"Congratulations, old man," Henry said heartily, patting him on the back. "I'm sure you'll be a great CEO."

"What?"

Selena jumped in to pick up on Henry's cue. "Yes," she added with new enthusiasm. "I think you'll do wonderfully as the head of our family business."

"Wait a second," Trader said impatiently. "I'm not firing you, Selena. We still need someone to run the company. I don't have time, obviously. I'm supposed to be playing football, remember?"

"You can't fire me," she laughed. "I've already quit."

"But you can't!"

"Why not?" she asked coolly. She was beginning to enjoy this. Trader was going to get a taste of his own medicine, and she wanted to watch as every bitter drop went down.

Trader began to flounder. "But what about your father's company?" he demanded rather desperately. "You can't just—just walk away from it!"

She patted his arm and smiled icily. "Oh, no? Just watch me." She gave his arm a little squeeze. "I leave it all in your eminently capable hands. And remember, all those clients of yours who bought stock in the company will want you to continue keeping Derringer profitable." She turned to her brother and grinned. "Well, Henry, I'm through putting in twelve-hour days. Now I'll let the new chairman of the board handle that responsibility."

"I can't run a company and also play football," Trader protested. But Selena paid no attention to him.

"What *are* you going to do, Selena?" Henry asked curiously.

"Oh, I've got my future mapped out for me. As a matter of fact, I'm going to take a piece of advice that Trader gave me."

Trader looked at her wildly, clearly wondering what that might be.

"I'm going to loosen up!" she announced gaily. "From now on, business will be more than a bunch of facts and figures for me." She gave them both a brilliant smile. "Yes," she went on. "You made an excellent suggestion."

"Just what are you driving at, anyway?" he asked suspiciously. "What suggestion did I make? All I said was that you should expand your horizons."

"You said I should get involved with the Aces, and that's exactly what I'm going to do."

"Be more specific, Selena," Henry added. "I'm still in charge of the Aces, you know."

But Selena only smiled coyly and, picking up the box from her desk, trotted out of the room. "Rah, rah, guys," she said as she twirled her index finger in the air. "I think I'll take over that cheerleading squad after all. It sounds like the perfect thing for me."

As Henry and Trader both gazed at her in astonishment, she sailed out the door, stopping only once to turn back and wink at them.

"Go, Aces!" she said with mock sweetness. And then *she* was gone.

Selena stood at the far end of the stadium behind the goalpost, effectively hidden as she watched the practice drill. Two leaden weeks had passed, and although she had not been idle, she couldn't restrain her curiosity any longer. As far as she knew, Trader had indeed been running Derringer Industries. He had to be worn to a frazzle, but she wanted to see for herself. She had told herself repeatedly that everything between them was over, that he was a heartless user and that she was better off without him. This argument sounded logical and sound, but the memory of his devastating blue eyes and the way they had looked inside her soul continued to torment her like a persistent demon.

She had distracted herself, however, with a new development that was sure to catch his attention, and it was marching across the field at this very moment. She suppressed her mirth as she watched the men's reactions.

"Who is that?"

"What is that?"

Tank Larson and Killer Miller stopped doing their push-ups and stared dumbfounded across the field.

Coming toward them was the biggest and broadest woman they had ever seen. She was wearing gray sweat pants and a sweat shirt with the letters CCCP emblazoned on it. A whistle hung on a lariat around her neck, and she was wearing real cleats.

"I'm in love," Killer said, slapping his heart in jest.

"Dig them sexy thighs. Damn, they're bigger than mine."

A group of players who had been doing sit-ups remained sitting up in a stupor as the giantess passed.

Even Trader, who never missed throwing a football through the tire hoop, missed completely when the woman came into his view. The ball took a few bounces and landed a few feet from her. Stopping suddenly, she reached down and scooped it up, moving into a perfect pass back to him. Trader caught it and looked around at his teammates, who all shrugged back at him.

The only one who hadn't seen her was the coach, who was busy diagramming plays on a blackboard near the benches. Suddenly noticing the huge shadow blocking his light, Eli nonchalantly pushed the woman away as though she were one of his players.

"You're in my light, son," he said without taking his eyes from the board. "There," he smiled happily, patting the blackboard. "Now, there's a great football play. What do you think?"

"Is not bad." The woman's husky, Russian-accented voice shattered his concentration. "But it is mistake to allow no defense for quarterback. Too risky."

Eli looked up wildly and jumped back a full three feet. "Who the—I mean—"

"Olga Vazaris," she announced, standing with her huge hands on her hips. "Newly hired coach." She extended a hand to Eli, but not to shake it. "Give chalk, if you please."

"Huh?" Eli gaped.

Olga took a piece of chalk and studied the board for several seconds while everyone gathered around her, the practice drills forgotten. "Aah," she said triumphantly. "Here is the problem." She redrew a few lines on the board and Eli nodded, transfixed.

"Not bad," he said. "I have to admit, it's not bad at all, but, uh—did I hear you say 'coach'?"

"Cheerleading coach!" Selena explained, marching into the group. She was wearing a clinging T-shirt and red gym shorts, and the players couldn't help staring at her. She pretended to ignore them, but she was keenly aware of Trader's presence. "Olga and I handpicked the best cheerleaders we could find to help promote the Aces and team spirit."

"Awwriiight!!" Killer smacked his hands together. "Cheerleaders! Let's see 'em!"

A piercing shrill of a whistle sounded, making everyone jump as Olga commanded their attention. They watched in fascination as out of the stadium exits came the cheerleaders. Unfortunately, and to the great disappointment of the players, the cheerleaders were not quite what they had expected.

"They're all men!" Killer exclaimed, startled. "What's going on here?"

Grumbles and sarcastic remarks followed as the men booed the bouncy group of cheerleaders—an energetic gathering of young, eager men who proceeded to do handstands and turn cartwheels. Trader cut through the players and took Selena's arm. His touch made her blood jump, and her heart contracted when she saw the weary lines and the dark circles under his eyes, but she kept her face composed as she turned to him.

"Yes?" she asked coolly.

"What is going on?" he asked tersely. "I was talking about women cheerleaders. Our fans like women."

"What about your women fans?"

"Selena," Trader said, irritated. "I want women, too."

"Oh," Selena said, poker-faced. "So I should add some females to the squad to balance it out, huh?"

Before Trader and the men could react, Olga blew the whistle again. Out of the stands came the rest of the cheerleading squad, a bunch of long-limbed young women dressed in revealing practice outfits.

As the female members of the squad joined the first group, the football players all applauded and whistled loudly. Trader shook his head at Selena.

"Very clever," he said. "But I'm not sure—" He stopped dead when he saw Olga staring daggers at him. She said nothing, standing with her arms folded, but the force of her presence was enough to melt a stone. "Uh, that is—"

"You do not like male cheerleaders?" Olga boomed. "And why not? Are you not equal-opportunity employer?"

"Well, of course," he said, "it's just that—"

"Good. Then we shall continue as planned." Olga nodded confidently, as if the matter had been settled.

Trader started to say something, but evidently thought better of it. "Okay, you guys, the show's over. Back to work. Ladies—" he started to say to the cheerleaders. He realized his mistake and added, "and gentlemen." They all looked at him expectantly as he gestured toward the indoor gymnasium under the stands. "If you don't mind. The team can't handle the distractions."

Again the shrill whistle sounded, forcing Trader to cover his ears.

"Is time to practice," Olga commanded. "Everyone to get from stadium and follow me inside."

In marked time, the cheerleaders marched, girl and boy, side by side, as they followed the imposing woman across the field and through a double set of doors under the stands.

Trader was still standing next to Selena, and she realized that she was going to have to say something to him. "So how's it going, Mr. Chairman? I haven't seen you for over two weeks now." A masterpiece of understatement, she thought sadly. She didn't add that she had been thinking about him constantly.

Trader limbered up his elbow a little and looked out at the players on the field. Her heart took a dive. Obviously, he wasn't concerned about her. He wasn't even looking at her. "Oh, I put in a good seven hours of practice every day," he said. "Then the bunch of us head down to the office to make sure Derringer is still solvent."

"The bunch of you?" Selena repeated cautiously.

Trader shrugged. "I couldn't do it all by myself. But, together, we're managing."

"I see." Her voice sounded pained, and she thought desperately of a way to capture his attention and hold it. "Look, Trader..."

He glanced down at her. "Yes?" So he wasn't going to make this any easier. His tone was as hard as nails.

"I—I just wondered how you were getting along, that's all," she finished lamely.

"Oh, you were, were you?" His eyes were flinty and cold, and she took a step back. "Well, it's not your concern anymore, is it? You made that quite clear. If you think you can waltz by now just to check up on things, forget it. It's too late for that."

"Hey, Trader!" Killer rescued her by bounding over and draping an arm around Trader. "We're having another poker game. Same time as last night. We want a chance to win back some of our money." Killer turned to Selena and smiled, unaware of the heated exchange he had interrupted. "Hi," he said amiably.

"Don't you people ever sleep?" she blurted out, wanting to sink into the ground the moment she said it. What Trader did at night was hardly her concern.

"I do now," Trader explained as he gestured at

Killer. "With all the extra work I have, I needed my own room. Now the goon squad doesn't keep me up."

Killer grinned affably, but Selena knew a barb when she heard one. So he *was* working himself to the bone. She should have felt a sense of satisfaction—that had been part of her plan, after all—but the sight of his haggard face only made her feel like dissolving into tears. Trader clearly wanted no sympathy from her, however.

"Well, it looks like you're quite capable of juggling two jobs," Selena said stiffly.

"Hey, Trader." It was Eli. "Let's get going. I want two miles of running, right now."

"Got to go," he said with a distinct air of relief that cut her more than his hasty words. "Duty calls. So long." He ran off without a backward glance. Selena's heart contracted as she watched him go, but she wasn't ready to give up. She had one more plan in mind.

That night, Selena gingerly made her way along the dormitory hallway under the stadium, peeking past the half-open doors to catch glimpses of the reclining bodies of huge football players. One lazy giant was lying on his bed reading a paper, and Selena called to him.

"Which is Trader O'Neill's room?" she asked.

The player gestured with a thumb. "Mr. Poker Face is three doors down. Just listen for the sound of losers moaning," he said.

She found the room, knocked bravely and waited as footsteps approached and the door was opened.

"Hey!" The startled face that greeted her was Tank's. "Look who's here!"

She peered inside, expecting to find an all-male bastion of card players, cigar smoke, and beer. Sure enough, there were Trader, Killer Miller, and Tank, but to her everlasting surprise, Olga Vazaris sat at the head of the rickety card table. She stepped inside and looked at Trader tentatively, hoping to find a receptive greeting.

He looked up sharply. "What are you doing here, Selena?" he asked directly. "Dropping by to check up on us?"

So he was going to be difficult. "Uh, no," she stalled. "As a matter of fact, I—" She eyed the empty seat across from him. "I . . . just thought I'd play a few rounds."

"The more the merrier," Tank boomed, gesturing toward the empty space. She slipped into it, avoiding Trader's eyes as Olga promptly and efficiently dealt out the cards.

"Five-card-draw poker," Olga announced. "One-eyed jacks shall be wild."

Selena thought back quickly to the poker games she had played in college. She was pretty rusty, but she was willing to have a go at it. She sensed that camaraderie was of the essence here. To back out now would make her look like a wet blanket.

Trader placed a stack of chips in front of her. "The white chips are ten dollars, the blues are twenty-five, and the reds are a hundred," he explained crisply.

She gulped. The last time she had played poker—several years before—the stakes had all been under a dollar.

"Ante in?" Killer said to Selena. He gestured for her to toss in a white ten-dollar chip.

She remembered belatedly that each player was supposed to put a chip in before the game started. Before she could comply, Trader reached across the table and did it for her. She looked up at him and caught the blue glint that had unnerved her so many times before. This time she almost wanted to be unnerved, wanted anything to happen that would bring back communication between them.

"She's in," he announced, his voice like steel.

Olga dealt out five cards face down, and Selena, after watching everyone else, picked them up and looked at her hand without showing anyone else what she had.

"Twenty-five," Trader said, and threw a blue chip into the center of the table.

"Me, too," Killer said, adding his money.

"And me," Tank added.

They all looked expectantly at Selena, who was too rattled to think clearly. Not only was she hastily trying to recall the poker hands she hadn't thought of in years, but she was trying to quell the rapid beating of her heart. She swallowed and studied her cards. Then, with a brave smile, she tossed in five red chips. At that moment, she remembered that the red chips were a hundred dollars each.

Like magic, the other players immediately began to drop out.

"I'm out."

"Me, too."

"Whatever she's got," Olga said, "I do not wish to bet five hundred dollars against."

Only Trader remained reticent. He looked at her shrewdly and thought for a second. "You're bluffing,"

he said. "You've got to be." He studied his hand. "I
can always tell when someone is bluffing me. They
can't look me straight in the eye." As he spoke, he
made deliberate eye contact with Selena. She willed
herself to remain calm as a bolt of awareness shot
through her. Did he really care about the card game?
She certainly didn't. All she could think of was the
way his hands had felt on her body, and the way his
magical eyes had captured her and thrilled her with
the depth of their response.

"Okay, I'm in." He placed the appropriate chips
into the pile and the game continued.

"How many cards for you, Selena?" Olga asked.

Selena glanced at her hand to determine if she was
going to exchange any cards for better ones. One look
at Trader made her retreat back to her cards.

"None," she said feebly, to everyone's apparent
amazement. "These are pretty good."

"Oh, man," Killer said, slapping his head. "Now
I know I was right to stay out of this hand."

"Two for me," Trader said, adding darkly, "I still
think she's bluffing."

"It is your turn to bet," Olga said.

Trader's eyes bored into Selena's, and for a moment
she was too flustered to move. She looked at her hand
and took a deep breath. "Uh, I'll bet"—she studied
the chips on the table—"all of them."

No one said a word.

"Is there something the matter?" she asked breathlessly.

Trader squinted at her cunningly. "Why, no. What
should be the matter?" He reached out and counted
all the chips she was betting. "Twelve hundred dollars.
Hmm." He considered. "Okay, I'm in." That decision

completed, he pushed the remainder of his winnings for the night into the center of the table.

Selena stared. Everyone waited. "Do I show my cards now?" she asked after a long pause.

"It would help," Trader said, the sudden glint in his eyes telling her plainly that he was onto her.

Selena turned her cards over so that everyone could see them. There was another, longer hush.

Tank was the first to speak. "Three queens," he announced. "I'm glad I folded."

"So much for the bluff," Killer agreed. He looked at Trader. "Can you beat that, little buddy?"

Trader tossed his cards down on the table and shook his head. "You win," he said gruffly to Selena.

"I do?" she asked weakly. Then a broad smile lit up her face. This wasn't so bad at all. All right, so blind luck had stepped in to aid her on the first hand. But her confidence mushroomed with her unwitting success, as remembered poker ploys from her college years swam suddenly back into her memory. She wanted to see Trader, and if this was the only way, she might as well play. When in Rome . . . , she thought, gearing up for the next hand.

But she lost the next few rounds, and so did everyone else—to Olga. After a while Selena realized what the player down the hall had meant about the sounds of losers moaning. The conversation during the game all seemed to focus around who would be able to win a hand back from the Russian card whiz. Olga, it seemed, was no match for anyone there, and she took her winning streak quite matter-of-factly. By the time it was her turn to deal, Selena's stack of chips was as depleted as everyone else's. Olga's looked like a miniature skyscraper.

"Well, I have much good luck tonight so far, yes?" she boomed. "And the night is youthful."

"Time for a comeback," Tank said, eyeing her strongly.

At least the mood had changed, Selena thought. The men had accepted her, and she was no longer a threat. She was losing. Not as much as they were, but it meant that their card game was back to normal.

"My deal," Selena announced, shuffling the cards and dealing them out.

"I bet fifty," Olga said staunchly. Everyone sighed.

Suddenly, almost as if on cue, the conversation took a new turn.

"So what do we do about the Kaywall account?" Killer asked as he tossed in his chips.

Selena instantly perked up with interest. The Kaywall account was one of Derringer's largest customers. What could Killer possibly know about it?

"I told him I'd call him for his final order tomorrow," Tank responded nonchalantly as he added his chips to the pile. "I promised him an autographed football for his kid if he took an extra three tons by Wednesday."

Selena's eye widened, but she said nothing. An extra two tons was a lot of business. What were these clowns up to, anyway?

"Push it another two tons," Trader put in, almost making her choke. "Tell him we'll discount it by five percent." He placed two blue chips in the middle and then added a red one. "And I raise you one hundred."

Selena swallowed hard and watched them closely as they talked about her business—her former business. Apparently, things were surviving quite well without her. This gave her an odd feeling of relief mixed with regret that she had walked out so suddenly. But mostly it gave her a burning curiosity to know more.

"I take two cards," Olga announced as she discarded a pair from her hand.

"How are you coming with that in-group project I put you in charge of?" Trader asked as Killer tossed three cards out. Selena was all ears again. What in-group project?

"I checked out a new location for that upstate warehouse." Killer picked up three new cards, and after looking at them, threw the hand face-down on the table in disgust.

She could stand it no longer. "Are you talking about our storage problem in mid-Atlantic distribution?" she asked nonchalantly as she gave Tank and Trader their cards.

"It's still a problem," Trader answered readily. It was the first civil thing he had said to her, and her hopes rose. But he looked at Tank, who gestured apologetically.

"First thing tomorrow," Tank said. "I promise. Eli had me doing laps, and I couldn't get down to the office in time to reach that real-estate agent."

"That's a major concern," Selena said, trying to sound casual, and failing. "You just can't wave it off. We've got over eighty tons that have to be distributed within the next month." She put her cards down and looked at Trader. "What's going on here? Don't tell me you've got Killer and Tank handling a multimillion dollar project."

"Okay, I won't tell you," Trader said flatly. "Whose bet is it?"

"It is mine," Olga said. She stole an understanding

look at Selena before placing three red chips neatly down on the table.

Everyone folded, including Selena, and Olga raked in the money once again. "I was bluffing," she informed them with a hearty Russian laugh. "I had nothing!"

Killer was thoroughly disgruntled as he dropped his cards onto the table. "And I folded with a pair of aces!"

Selena wasn't even listening. Her eyes were focused on Trader. "Trader..." she said tentatively, willing him to look at her, to accept the truce she was silently offering.

Her tone was so beseeching that Olga's head snapped up and surveyed the situation in a glance. "Okay, game is over," she announced abruptly as she scooped up all the chips.

"How come?" Tank asked plaintively, blissfully unaware of what had just transpired. "You just can't quit all of a sudden."

Killer chimed in. "Yeah, you got to give us a chance to win our money back. What happened to 'the night is youthful'?"

"Night is youthful, but Olga is not getting any younger. I need my beauty sleep. Come," she announced, but it was more of a command. "Cash me in, we all go now. We leave these two alone."

Comprehension belatedly dawned on the faces of the players as Selena stared at Olga, who was busily putting the chips away. Olga looked up and caught her eye with a twinkle.

Selena took a deep breath. "Thank you all for letting me play," she said evenly. "I had a lovely time."

Everyone filed out of the room, leaving Selena very much alone with Trader. She turned and faced him, her heart jumping with anticipation, her eyes glossy with hope.

- 9 -

SHE WAS ABOUT to speak when suddenly Trader threw back his head and burst out laughing.

"What's so funny?" Selena demanded nervously.

Trader regarded her wryly as he ran a hand through his thick black hair. "Oh, everything." He shrugged. "But I'm glad you came by to see me."

Some instinct told her not to give everything away at once. She feigned surprise. "See you? Don't be silly. Why should I come to see the man who stole my company?"

"You're right. Why should you?"

"I was looking for Olga," Selena explained unconvincingly. "We have to go over a new cheerleading routine for the opening game next week, and I was told that she was still in the stadium."

Trader walked over to the door and opened it. "She went thataway," he said, gesturing with his thumb. "If you hurry, you can still catch her."

Selena actually got up and headed for the doorway. This was not going at all the way she had imagined. But when she reached the door, Trader slammed it shut and grabbed her around the waist.

"Let go of me," she protested. "I didn't come here to wrestle with a jock."

"You didn't come here to see Olga, either."

She refused to fight him, but his grip was as powerful as ever. "I could kill you," she said.

"But you won't. I think you came here to tell me how sorry you are."

Selena forgot the calm, reasonable approach she had planned. "Why, you pig-headed, conceited oaf! Do you really think *I* need to apologize?"

He looked down at her keenly. "Selena Derringer, you came here to see me. And I'm glad you did. Why deny it?"

"Okay," she said after a moment. "But I still haven't forgiven you."

"Fine. That makes two of us."

She let out a long, heavy sigh. "We could go around in circles forever, you know." He didn't answer, but the silence that followed was not an uncomfortable one, she realized after a while. And she was still standing locked in his arms, which was a definite improvement from that afternoon on the field. "You're very stubborn," she observed finally.

"So are you." He smiled slightly and changed his hold on her. It was still firm, but no longer threatening.

All at once his arms became the familiar, enticing haven she wanted them to be, and she wished fervently that the stumbling blocks between them would vanish.

"I've missed you," he murmured into her hair, and a part of her began to melt. She hadn't been sure if he even wanted to see her again. His tender admission was like honey to her soul.

When his mouth descended to coax her into a kiss, she complied willingly, letting him overpower her just for one stolen moment. This wouldn't solve anything, she knew. But it was such sweet release after the weeks of tormenting disappointment...

Their mouths met in a gentle rush of fire. Before long, their tongues were hungrily intertwined, and they were swept away into a whirlwind of feeling. "Oh, Trader!" Selena cried brokenly when his mouth lifted from her, but he never let her get any further, for he took her mouth again in a savage burst of desire that left her limp.

Trader lifted her and carried her the few steps to the bed. Her eyes flew open in alarm. "No," she said weakly, but he only kissed her again and stroked her hair with such tenderness that tears sprang to her eyes. "This won't help," she tried to say, but Trader hushed her as his knowing hands slipped under her thin cotton T-shirt.

"Oh, yes it will," he whispered fervently. "Trust me, Selena. This is exactly what we needed all along."

She knew she should object. They needed to talk more, to sort out their differences logically and fairly. But how could she think about logic when his tongue was burning a trail across her throat, and his strong hands were lifting the flimsy shirt over her head? In another moment, his mouth sought the firm softness of her breasts, and she could do nothing to stop the erotic moan that escaped her parted lips.

A little smile of pleasure darted across his irregular features as he watched her. "Ah, you want me, Selena. You can't deny it." He drew one rosy nipple into his mouth and sucked it gently. Her eyes closed in passion as she savored the rush of feeling. "Admit it, honey," he breathed roughly. "Say you want me."

"I want you!" she cried, her hands gripping the coarse shock of black hair that hovered at her breast. "And I'm lost..."

He could not have known what she meant by those last words, and it was just as well, she thought dimly. His eyes sparked with blue lights as he sat up and quickly removed the loose athletic clothing he wore, revealing the hard planes of his glorious body. Selena's eyes traveled hungrily over every masculine inch. How could she ever have thought that she could forget him? It was hopeless. The man had cast a spell on her, and she was his willing captive.

He stretched out beside her on the bed with the confidence and inherent power of a lion. In another moment, his hands slid her skimpy shorts down her legs, and they were together again, as melded and in harmony as they had been that wonderful night in the Berkshires. Trader smiled at her, a tiny, private smile that seemed to convey a wealth of intimacy.

"You look so beautiful lying there for me," he said softly. "Like a perfect painting come to life."

Selena stretched out her arms and gathered him close to her. She wanted to hold him as tightly as she could, to blot out the painful memories of the last few

weeks and start anew. They kissed again and again,
teasing and tempting each other into a frenzy of need.
His hands found and mastered the feminine contours
of her body and she yielded silently, letting him take
all that she had to give.

His mouth teased her breasts once again, bringing
them to an aching fullness and then descending to the
gentle mound of her stomach. Everywhere he touched
her a little bonfire blazed, and her hips moved rest-
lessly on the bed, unconsciously encouraging him.

She gave a little cry when his hand slipped between
her silken thighs, stroking them possessively before
seeking the tender flesh inside that proclaimed her
womanhood. Then she was lost completely in the
warm swirling sensations that sang through her body.
Her face glowed with pleasure as he brought her to a
peak of desire.

But he withdrew before she could pass into oblivion
and covered her soft body with his. "Love me," she
murmured passionately, needing with all her body and
soul for the words to transcend the mere physical act
of love.

She was more than ready for him; he slid into her
effortlessly in one single line of flowing electricity.
They waited for a moment as her body molded itself
around him. Then the erotic rhythm began, slowly at
first, as each nerve-ending responded to the friction.
Before long, they passed into a new, timeless stretch
in which all barriers between them faded, and they
joined into one.

"How perfectly we fit together," she marveled
aloud. He shuddered slightly in her arms, and she
wondered if he had caught her unintentional double

meaning. But words were lost as the crescendo spiraled, and they sailed together to the crest of the great wave that claimed them.

Selena was overwhelmed at the shattering enormity that engulfed her. All earthly constraints dropped away from her as she hurtled toward one single dominant truth: Trader O'Neill had claimed her, and she belonged to him. She knew that now as simple and inevitable fact. As they lay entwined in the aftermath of passion, she accepted it silently. She was in love with Trader, and there was nothing she could do about it. It was much too late to turn back.

Her eyes opened to the new reality. Everything was the same: the small, neat room, the moonlight peeking through the one window, the silhouette of Trader's body nestled comfortably against hers. But everything was irrevocably different.

What had she done? She had lost her heart like a schoolgirl, surrendering to the magic of his touch without any kind of commitment or solace from him. She turned her head away in dismay.

"Hey," he whispered, turning her head back to his shoulder. "What's the matter?"

The revelation was too new to hide. "Will you still love me tomorrow?" she blurted out ruefully, quoting the line from an old song.

He chuckled. "Oh, is that all? Sure," he answered gamely. "Why not?" He nuzzled her ear. "I'll definitely love your body, if that's what you mean."

Selena suppressed a heavy sigh. Her worst suspicions were confirmed. "Trader . . ." she began bravely, trying to hold back the tide of love she was afraid was shining in her eyes. He looked at her expectantly.

"You see, that didn't really solve anything, did it?"

"Don't be so sure," he said gravely. "I'm willing to admit one thing."

Her heart leaped. "What's that?"

"I'm going out of my mind at the office," he stated grimly. "Your revenge plan worked. I need you there, Selena. I can't possibly handle it on my own. Another week of this, and I would have lost my mind."

Well, that was definitely better than nothing. She smiled a little in the dark. "I'll see what I can do," she promised. Then she nudged him. "What about Killer and Tank and the guys? I thought they were helping you. It sounded before like you had things pretty well under control."

"That was just a front," he admitted with a clear air of relief that he could now tell the truth. "They know how I felt about your leaving, and they knew I didn't want to admit to you how much I needed you."

Selena thought for a long moment. This was definitely a step. Trader had never before admitted anything like this to her. "Are you saying you'd like to compromise?" she asked carefully.

"That's exactly what I'm saying," he said eagerly.

"Congratulations."

"For what?"

"I believe this is a first. The great O'Neill is actually asking for help. And what's more, ladies and gentlemen, he's actually settling for a compromise. I propose a moment of silence." She lightened her words with jest, but they both knew she meant what she said. They were actually quiet for a minute, and then Trader spoke.

"Will you come by the office tomorrow?" he asked hopefully.

She couldn't resist the clear note of appeal in his voice. "Okay."

"What time?" he pressed.

"After cheerleading practice is over." She was thoroughly enjoying her temporary advantage. Maybe Trader wasn't in love with her, but at least he needed her—for now.

Selena marched down the familiar hallway the next day, feeling as if she had only been on a pleasant vacation. But when she reached her former office, she saw that her absence had indeed resulted in some major changes, and that nothing would ever go back to the way it had been before.

She stood unnoticed in the doorway, watching the disconcerting scene. Killer and Tank were hovered over the file cabinet like two giants surrounding an anthill. They were poring through the files in fruitless pursuit of something, and random papers and folders were spilling out of corners and falling to the floor.

The rest of the office looked like disaster. There were stacks of papers everywhere, sitting on desks, piled on the floor, covering chairs, and even tacked haphazardly to the walls. Trader was on the phone, nodding intently as he scribbled notes onto a yellow pad, snapping his fingers at Killer and Tank to hurry up whatever they were doing.

"That's right, Mr. Conklin," Selena heard him say. She knew he was talking to the crusty head of one of Derringer's biggest accounts. "I'm just looking over your latest order right now." Again Trader snapped his fingers frantically until he saw Selena standing at the door.

Without batting an eye, she whipped the file from the right drawer and marched over to the desk. "Give me the phone," she commanded.

"With pleasure." Trader put it right in her hand, and she went to work immediately.

"Hello, Hank? It's Selena; what can I do for you?" She motioned for Trader to get out of her seat, which he did at once, and Selena resumed her old position as easily as if nothing had changed. "I'm looking at your order right now," she continued smoothly, keeping the frown out of her voice. "Some idiot left out a zero. That's the usual hundred tons, right?"

"A hundred tons!" Killer slapped his forehead, and looked at Tank. "Holy cow," he said. "That order you showed me last week was right after all."

Selena motioned frantically for Killer to stop talking. "What? Oh, that was nothing, Hank, just one of our secretaries who mixed up an order. I'll tell him to be more careful next time... Same to you Hank, and thanks for understanding." Selena hung up the phone and looked at the group around her with unconcealed pride. "Any other problems?" she quipped.

"Hey, now," Killer said defensively. "You can't blame me. This is volunteer work, charity, you know what I mean? I was only trying to help."

"Yeah, me, too," Tank added. "If you want to blame anyone, talk to this guy." He jerked a thumb at Trader.

Trader stood leaning against the file cabinet. "It was an honest mistake. Would you care to continue here, Selena? You seem to be doing better than all of us put together."

She wasted little time. "I want those files back in order," she commanded, and Tank and Killer responded with a salute.

"You got it, boss," Tank said as he began shoveling paper with his huge hands.

"Barry!" She called for her secretary, but there was no answer. "Barry?"

Trader shrugged. "I think he's still down in the warehouse checking on a shipment."

"We have a computer for that," Selena said and spun around to face the terminal. There was no response as the screen remained blank. "What's going on here?"

"It's being fixed," Trader explained as he gestured to Killer. "He accidently spilled some coffee on it and shorted it out. That's why we've had to resort to the files."

She shook her head and pointed to the door. "Killer, take the Conklin file down there and make sure they forward the shipping information to our midwestern warehouse. And tell Barry to hightail it back here on the double." Next, she turned to Trader. "Where are we in the upstate battle for storage?" she asked without missing a beat.

"Nowhere," he said. "I've been trying a real-estate agent in—"

"Forget agents," Selena said flatly. She flipped through her Rolodex and, a second later, was talking to one of her distributors upstate. "George, this is Selena Derringer. I want you to rent out a warehouse with about twenty thousand square feet by the end of the week."

The call ended in a matter of minutes and she turned back to her audience.

"Well, that was easy," Trader said, impressed.

"Running this company is like running a football team," Selena explained. "Its not just a question of calling the shots. You have to know whom to delegate to. It's called management."

"I was never good at management," Trader observed candidly.

"You don't have to look so proud of that," she retorted. "You can't do everything yourself when you're the boss. You have to share things. And compromise." The word hit her smack in the face as she recalled the intimate way in which she had used it with him the night before. Flushing, she looked up to see if he had caught it, but his face was a mask of control.

She was rescued by Barry, who came bustling in at that moment, almost tripping over Tank. His face lit up when he saw her, but his pleasure was short-lived.

"Don't get too excited, Barry," Selena warned. "I'm just housecleaning."

"Heaven knows, we can use a good cleaning," Barry said. "Our Brooklyn factory can't handle the load of new orders we've been getting recently."

"New orders?" Selena was puzzled. "What new orders?"

As she spoke, Barry handed her a weighty sheaf of papers from the bottom of her desk. She flipped through them in amazement.

"There're over two hundred thousand tons here! But how?"

Trader sat down in her seat and beamed. "I may not be a great manager, but I am a great salesmen. And it doesn't hurt when the buyers know I'm the new quarterback for the Aces. That's gotten me more orders than you can imagine."

"He's been giving away free football tickets with every order," Barry added excitedly. "And it works.

He's great at it. Our customers all want to come in and see Tank and Killer here, and Trader just takes the orders down. They don't expect football heroes to get on the phone and take orders."

They were all watching her to see if she would mind, as if the dignity of the company might somehow be at stake, but Selena absorbed this new information with considerable grace. "I see," she said at last. "Well, if it works, use it."

"So what do you say we work as a team?" Trader asked immediately, his confident grin returning.

Selena didn't answer, but she spent the rest of the afternoon getting things back in order. It wasn't that Trader's new staff was really so inept, it was that they didn't have the time or the real inclination to handle the business properly. Trader himself was as perceptive and capable as he had been that day he had helped her with the financial statements, but his time and energy were limited. She could sense that the physical exertion was affecting him more than the other men, and Selena remembered with a jolt that he was, after all, an old man to be playing football. It had been easy to forget that in light of his recent successes— and in the powerful strength of his arms. But there was still a lot to take care of, and by five o'clock, she was exhausted.

"That's it; I've had it. You're back on course," she announced, kicking off her shoes and falling back in her chair.

Trader's eyes held hers for a long moment, and the night they had spent together came back to her in a rush. "I knew you wouldn't abandon your father's company."

Selena looked down. She had managed to avoid this topic all afternoon. Now she had to tell him the truth. "You don't understand, Trader. I didn't come here today to take over. I came because you asked me to."

His eyes flickered. "Does that mean you're not coming back?"

She hesitated. "I'll pinch-hit until we find a replacement," she offered. "I'm not going to jeopardize the company or the team. But after that, I'll be moving on." He looked stricken suddenly, and she hastened to explain. "You were right," she said earnestly. "This really wasn't for me. I was only doing it out of a sense of obligation. I—I've got something else lined up now."

"I see." His voice was dry and expressionless, and she could almost see him retreating into a shell. "Well, if your mind is made up . . ."

She wanted to reach out and take his hand, to stroke his cheek, to put her arms around him and hold him. But he looked so inscrutable suddenly, as if he were a million miles away. Why did this uninvited wall always spring up between them? Why couldn't the precious intimacy they could create exist between them all the time? Selena frowned in frustration, and Trader immediately stepped back, his face blank.

The phone rang, shattering the moment.

Barry's voice came over the intercom. "That was Olga Vazaris," he said. "She called to say she'll meet you for dinner at the Duchess's at eight tonight."

"The Duchess's?" Trader repeated. "So you really liked it there."

"Yes," she answered, feeling a little sheepish.

Trader's influence on her had been so profound that she was even eating at his favorite restaurant. If the man couldn't see that, he must be dense. Couldn't he also see that she had fallen in love with him? She willed herself to keep the longing from her eyes and gathered her things together slowly. Obviously, he would make a move now if he wanted to. But he just stood there looking at her with that infuriatingly cool expression.

"I—I'll see you later," Selena said finally, stepping back into her shoes. With a barely concealed sigh, she mustered her dignity and walked out, leaving him standing behind in the office.

"Y'all sit down now, and I'll fatten you up with some corn bread," the Duchess announced as Selena appeared. It was early, only six-thirty, but Selena had looked forward to the comfort and anonymity of the Duchess's place before the dinner crowd livened it up. To her surprise, Olga was there ahead of her, somberly drinking a straight vodka as if it were water.

Selena approached, wondering how the older woman always managed to look as if she were holding court. "You are pale," Olga observed as Selena sank into a chair. "Something troubles you, no?"

"Something troubles me, yes," Selena admitted readily. "That Trader is enough to drive anyone crazy."

"What?" The Duchess overheard this dispirited remark and bustled over with a pitcher of sangria. "Here, honey, you drink some of this. Now what's that about my boy Trader?"

"He is no boy," Olga objected stonily. "For football, he is an old man. And still he has much to learn."

"Maybe he's just not very interested," Selena mumbled into her drink. "And he doesn't know that he's hurting other people." She didn't add that the other person in question was her, but she didn't have to.

Olga raised an eyebrow and exchanged a pointed glance with the Duchess.

"That boy never hurt nobody," the Duchess said, shaking her head emphatically so that the gold hoops danced on either side of her broad face. "Not on purpose. If you want him, honey, you got to go after him."

The Duchess didn't know the half of it, and Selena was in no mood to explain. "I've done everything I can," she said. "He only needs me around to run the company. And to go to bed with." She added the last phrase in such a low voice that she wasn't sure the two women had heard, but they had.

"Aha," Olga said at once. "Now I see the problem. The problem, *petrushka*, is with you."

Selena looked up sharply, and Olga took this as an invitation to continue. "You think he should speak up, yes? But he will not. And do you know why?" Selena shook her head, curious in spite of herself. "Because he is too stupid to know how!" Olga finished triumphantly.

"Trader isn't stupid," Selena retorted, surprised to find herself defending him.

"Oh, yes, he is," the Duchess put in unexpectedly. "Men usually are, don't you know. They just can't help themselves. That's why the good Lord created women's intuition. We got to step in and help those devils out sometimes, else they just go 'round in circles."

"She is correct," Olga chimed in. "If your man does not declare himself, it is up to you. Do not be afraid, darling," she added when she saw the look of dismay on Selena's face. "I promise you it will all go well. Have I not seen the way he looks at you? He is enraptured." She smiled serenely as Selena gazed at her in astonishment. Selena had never expected Olga to be the type to offer advice for the lovelorn, but then Olga was a self-proclaimed expert in practically everything, and she was seldom wrong about most things.

"Now, what you need is a nice batch of the Duchess's fried chicken," the Duchess decided, giving Selena a shrewd once-over. Selena knew better than to object. "And for you," she added, turning to Olga, "a big plate of spareribs, with some cole slaw on the side." She nodded in confirmation, pleased with her choices, but Olga intercepted her.

"No," Olga commanded sternly in a voice that would melt ice. "I shall have fried chicken also. But you may leave the cole slaw." Her laser glare made Selena sit up straight, and the Duchess regarded Olga with unaccustomed awe.

"Yes, ma'am," the Duchess answered swiftly, backing toward the kitchen, and Selena broke into delighted laughter.

- *10* -

THE FIRST PRE-SEASON game was heralded as the beginning of a new era, and once again, Brooklyn turned out in full force for the occasion. Selena and Henry rode to the stadium in the limousine, and Selena surprised her brother by dispensing with her customary business suit for once and wearing a bright red T-shirt that said "I'm an Ace!" and a pair of tight white jeans.

She was fluttering with excitement, and not just because of the game. She hadn't spoken to Trader since her conversation the day before yesterday with Olga and the Duchess, but she knew that today would present the opportunity. Her spirits were high despite the occasional lurch in her stomach. If Trader really cared for her, she was going to find out. She knew

he was stubborn, but so was she. She wasn't going
to give up without a fight.

They heard the roar of the crowd before they actually reached the stadium. The long, sleek car inched
its way past the hordes of people, the noisy traffic,
and the sidewalk vendors selling everything from bal-
loons and pennants to six-foot stuffed pandas and foot-
long hot dogs. The parking lot was even more con-
gested, but the driver skillfully wove his way up to
the entrance in a matter of minutes. Selena stepped
out into the brilliant sunshine and looked around ap-
prehensively. It was totally irrational, but she had the
uneasy feeling that Trader was going to materialize
right there in the parking lot.

"Come on," Henry said impatiently, like a child
tugging at his mother's sleeve. "Let's go."

She turned to her brother with an affectionate smile.
This day meant just as much to Henry as she hoped
it would for her. He had waited a long time for this
game. As they made their way through a private entrance, Selena realized she was just as excited. "What
kind of team are they playing against?" she asked
nervously.

"The Chargers, of course." Henry looked at his
sister as if she were completely dense. "Don't you
know who the Chargers are?"

Selena tried to look intelligent. "They must be a
pretty big adversary, right?"

"Super Bowl champs two years in a row," Henry
said pointedly. "They're number one, and unbeata-
ble."

"Oh. So we lost before the game starts, is that it?"

Henry laughed. "The Aces are a new team now,

with some great players. Besides, 'the game ain't over until it's over.'" Selena smiled quietly. The quote from Yogi Berra reflected more than today's game to her. It reminded her quite jarringly of her personal situation with Trader. As they were escorted along the private first-class seats over to the fifty-yard line, her heart began to beat faster in anticipation. She had been to very few football games in her life, and she had forgotten—or never really noticed—the amount of pageantry that went along with the game. "My God," she exclaimed, looking around. "Is this the same stadium we've been coming to all summer? It feels totally different."

The worn field had been transformed overnight. The lines were all a brilliant white, the grass had never looked greener, and the goalposts had been painted blue and gold. All over the stands, people waved banners and cheered anxiously as they awaited the players. It was like a Roman spectacle.

Suddenly, the loudspeaker boomed out, "Ladies and gentlemen! It is a great honor for me to introduce to you . . . the Brooklyn Aces!"

One by one, the announcer introduced each individual on the team, saving the star players for the end. Every time a name was called, a player ran through a double line of cheerleaders onto the field and bowed energetically to the crowd. When Killer Miller and Tank Larson were called, the crowd went wild, stamping their feet and chanting "Kill 'em! Kill em!" Even Selena was caught up in the fervor. Then there was a hushed silence.

"What's happening?" Selena asked Henry. "Is everything all right?"

Henry just smiled like a satisfied cat. "It's all planned. Just wait."

Suddenly, a new chant was started in the stands, one that began on one side and was answered by the other. At first Selena couldn't make out the words, but when the entire squad of cheerleaders took it up, she was electrified by the new realization. "Who's our Ace in the hole?" one side called. "Trader! Trader! Trader!" the other side responded. The dual chant continued, increasing steadily as the anticipation rose. Then there was a deafening roar as Trader came running onto the field, and for the first time Selena realized what his comeback meant to the fans. He lifted his arms in a victory salute, turning to face the crowd on all sides with an enormous grin. Waving and smiling at the fans for a long minute, he soaked in the enthusiastic response with obvious relish, clearly enjoying every second of the affection being lavished on him.

Henry leaned over and started to say something to Selena, but she was barely aware of Henry as she watched the outpouring of emotion being played out on the field. She had never really understood Trader's ambition, she realized at that moment. She had thought that he simply wanted to play football, to have his season in the sun. But as she watched, tears stinging her large brown eyes, she knew that *this* was his moment in the sun. He would never forget this reception—and neither would she.

As she turned once more to face the press box, his exuberant face caught hers and he looked straight at her. She knew that the look on her face said it all. Her heart was open wide at that moment, and she met his gaze with all the love and admiration that were welling up inside of her. Trader's eyes focused so keenly on her that she thought everyone in the entire stadium must be aware of the electricity between them. It was as if a direct line had sprung up between them, connecting them with its powerful but invisible force. Trying to blink back the tears, Selena succeeded only in increasing the intensity. She trembled under the power of Trader's spell, her hands gripping the railing in front of her as she basked in the light of his blue eyes.

The voice of the announcer broke into their silent exchange, and Trader broke away only when the two teams lined up for the national anthem. Selena was but dimly aware of the notes being sung. She was still trembling, and her eyes followed Trader's every move.

The game began noisily, each team hurtling itself against the other in an effort to gain a quick advantage. Selena learned that the quarterback was truly the anchor of the team as she watched Trader maneuver and plot the various plays. It was like watching an exquisitely timed dancer with extraordinary reflexes. With unrelenting speed and drive, the Aces moved the ball down the field under Trader's expert command. Selena found that she was actually holding her breath when they came close to scoring. Her joy was wild and abandoned when they triumphantly intercepted a pass, and her disappointment was acute when they lost the ball.

"Stop pouting, Selena." Henry laughed at his sister's reactions. "It's just a pre-season game. I'm surprised at how well they are doing."

"I can't help it, Henry. Every time Trader steps

back to throw, I want to punch those guys who are running to tackle him. I hope Tank and Killer keep protecting him."

"Me, too," Henry answered, looking at her with new eyes. "Me, too." But when the crowd roared at a play in which Trader completed a long pass, Henry was up and cheering with the rest of the crowd. "Kill 'em, Aces! Go, go!"

Selena looked at her brother and suddenly caught on to something—that uncontained enthusiasm that had always mystified her in sports fans. At last she understood. Suddenly, the fate of the Aces had become a matter of earth-shaking importance. She threw back her head and laughed recklessly. Then she was on her feet, yelling and screaming and throwing herself into the excitement. "Go! Go! Go! Go! Go!"

A few plays later, Trader took them within ten feet of the goal line, but he wasn't able to score.

"They're bringing in a kicker," Henry explained as the crowd chanted, "Field goal, field goal."

Selena understood. A kicker ran onto the field and the ball was hiked over the players toward him. He kicked it successfully over the goalpost as the other team tried to stop him, giving the Aces three points.

But the first half of the game ended on a downbeat note; the Aces were behind 7–3. In spite of this, the fans cheered wildly as the players left the field, and Selena saw that even Trader was beaming under his helmet. She was debating whether or not to try and find him during half-time, but then remembered that something else was planned for the break.

"Ladies and gentlemen," the announcer boomed, his voice reverberating with each phrase, "we are proud to present, for the first time anywhere, the Brooklyn Aces cheerleaders!" The crowd reacted with an uprush of glee as the cheerleading squad came bounding out onto the field, and recorded music blared through the stadium. Olga was stationed off to the side, watching her charges like a hawk, and they proceeded to go through their paces with disarming accuracy and style. Selena was delighted with the results. She had never been completely sure if the cheerleaders were going to be a boon or an embarrassment, but thanks to the addition of the men and to Olga's sense of restraint, they turned out to be a definite advantage to the team.

The second half of the game began with renewed fanfare, and the Aces had to scramble to keep up. They fell even further behind when the Chargers scored another touchdown, putting the score at 14−3 for several agonizing minutes, but they recouped with another touchdown and a field goal, bringing them within a point of their competition, 14−13.

Selena found herself completely caught up in the excitement. She was still tingling with the look she and Trader had exchanged before the game, but now the game was everything, and she wanted the Aces to win with an ardor that surprised her. "Go, Aces!" she yelled as Trader bolted down the field, dodging the paths of two huge tackles. She knew enough about the game and about Trader by now to anticipate what would happen next. Sure enough, Trader twisted his body into the familiar pattern—the one he had demonstrated so brilliantly during the tryout, and the one that had once resulted in his injury long ago. Her heart stopped as he executed a stunning turn, running free toward the goal.

Then a scream rose and choked in her throat as one determined Charger, breaking free from the ranks, hurled his massive body through the air, directly in Trader's path. Trader bravely attempted another dodge, but the move had been too sudden, and his timing was off. He fell headlong into the opposing player's side, his entire body somersaulting helplessly and then striking the ground with a thud. The other player got up, but Trader remained motionless on the ground.

Selena lost all sense of propriety, all notion of time or place. Without thinking, she shot up and was about to run down from the bleachers, when Henry stopped her.

"Where do you think you're going?" he asked.

"Trader!" she cried, her voice high with fear, but Henry wouldn't let her go.

"He's all right," he said kindly. "The doc'll have a look at him."

"Doctor?" She watched as a medic and two of the referees sprinted onto the field and knelt by Trader's side. The doctor examined him and questioned him briefly, and some of Selena's hysteria diminished when she saw him nod and answer, obviously alert. The three men helped him up, and an overwhelming sense of relief flooded through her as she realized that she had overreacted. Trader was fine. The crowd cheered him back, and he went to the sidelines to rest for a moment.

Selena bit her lip and turned back to her seat. The depth of her response to his possible injury had shaken her. She hadn't realized just how much she cared for Trader, until now. The thought that he might be hurt, might be suffering in pain, had almost devastated her.

The love that had been warring within her rose up like a banner, calling to her and mocking her at the same time.

Within minutes, Trader was on the field again, and Henry's fingers closed around her arm. "He's okay, Selena," he said gently.

"I know," she whispered, subdued. She watched as Trader ignored the slight injury he had sustained in his shoulder and continued to play. His dedication was passionately clear. The game was everything to him; nothing would stop him from playing it as hard and as well as he could. Selena watched him anxiously. She knew that there was something between them, no matter how unresolved, but was it going to be enough? Was there room in Trader's life for anything but the dream that had driven him for so long, a dream that had propelled him to take over her company and manipulate her life?

She didn't know. She continued to wonder as the game continued, the players battling each other with frenzied, driven looks on their streaked faces. Their husky, masculine bodies fought with a ferocious intensity, leaving no room for a thought or regard for anything else.

In the last few minutes of the game, the score was still 14–13. With only twenty seconds left to play, Trader threw a long pass that put the Aces about thirty yards from the goalpost.

"They'll never make it," Henry said pessimistically. "It's time for another field goal. Bring in the kicker!" he called.

The clock was now stopped with ten seconds left to play. Trader walked off the field and was replaced by the field-goal kicker. There was a hush as they waited for the final play to determine the winner of the game. Selena watched as the ball was hiked back and lined up for the kicker. She heard the sound of boot against ball, and then the missile was sent soaring between the goalposts for a three-point score.

"We won! We won!" Henry was dancing and screaming in the stands with everyone else.

Selena couldn't help being caught up in the exultation as the fans went wild, throwing streamers into the air and pouring down from the stands to vent their joy on the field. Henry was as exhilarated as a kid at a birthday party. He grabbed her and lifted her, twirling her in the air with a cry of pure happiness.

"I did it!" he shouted, throwing his arms open wide. He gave Selena a resounding smack and disappeared into the stands, climbing up to the press box for a victorious press conference.

Selena hesitated and then chose the opposite direction, heading toward the locker room. Elbowing her way through the throngs of fans and reporters, she waited by the entrance, knowing that Trader was bound to appear. He popped out unexpectedly, newly showered and already dressed, ready to face the eager questions and autograph books that surrounded him. Selena watched him with a sudden sense of shyness. This was a new Trader, one who had become a celebrity overnight.

He handled the attention deftly, with the masterful ease that accompanied everything he did, but Selena detected an undercurrent of anxiety that she was sure only she could see. He made all the right moves, smiled at all the appropriate places, but she was sure that something was wrong.

He was signing his tenth autograph when he looked up suddenly and caught Selena's eyes on him.

"Congratulations," she ventured timidly. He looked confused, although she couldn't imagine why, and she added hastily, "On winning the game."

He gave a short laugh that sounded almost ironic. "Thanks," he said curtly, his eyes lingering on her face. Selena was flustered, but she continued undaunted. "I—I guess the old saying about how you can never go back isn't true in your case."

"You can't," he said flatly, shaking his head with a determination that aroused her curiosity even more. She sank back and watched as he hurriedly finished signing his last autograph. Then, without a word or a backward glance, he strode off, refusing to answer any more questions or to accept any more greetings.

"What the—" Selena dashed off after him, losing him in the crowd for a minute, but making it to the parking lot just in time to see his dark head disappear through the outer gate.

She felt like a spy as she followed him down one street and then another, wondering where he could be going after winning his first game. Somehow she wasn't surprised when she saw him duck into a local tavern. A little smile played around her lips as she slipped inside, her eyes searching him out in the crowd.

The bar was filled with fans who had just left the game, but Trader walked through them unaffected. He headed straight to the bar, where he sat down on a stool with a resolute expression on his face.

Selena approached him tentatively. She was trembling slightly, but she didn't care. Whatever was bugging him had something to do with her, whether he knew it or not. Of that much she was suddenly, irrevocably sure. In a flash, she knew that the Duchess had been right. Men didn't always know what was happening to their hearts. Sometimes they needed a nudge in the right direction. With renewed hope, she silently sat down on the stool next to his and rested her elbows on the bar with her chin in her hands.

Trader looked at her for a long minute. Then he crooked a finger at the bartender. "Five shots of tequila, please," he ordered.

The bartender lifted an eyebrow but complied silently, lining five shot glasses up on the bar and pouring the potent liquid into each one.

"Uh—just a club soda for me," Selena said quietly. She turned to Trader. She knew that her face was brimming with love, but she wasn't afraid to be vulnerable now. Trader needed her. Knowing that she was there for him made her unaccountably happy. She studied him for a moment and then said, "You're a sore winner."

His fingers toyed with the first shot of tequila, but he didn't drink it. "I have a rotten nature, you know that?" he asked suddenly.

She smiled a little. "Oh, I know."

"Nothing makes me happy. I finally got what I wanted, and it's not good enough." He didn't look at her, but his tone was beseeching her to pursue it, and she did.

"You're happy, Trader," she said. "You just don't recognize happiness when it hits you in the face."

He sighed wearily and shook his head. "It's all over for me."

"What are you talking about? You won the game, didn't you? You're a star now."

He swung around on the stool and faced her. "I won this game. And maybe the next game. But it's not going to last, Selena." He looked down and then back at her, his eyes challenging her in some way that she couldn't quite decipher. "I've already discussed it with Eli. It's only a matter of time."

She laughed. "You sound like you only have six months to live."

"No. But I can't play football much longer. I'll make it through the season, but that's it."

She still didn't get it. "So, what's wrong with that?" she asked gently. "What did you expect?"

He picked up the first shot and held it up to the light, turning it around in his hand as if to examine it. Selena waited. "It's been fifteen years," he said finally, so quietly that she had to lean forward to catch the words. The shot glass rattled back to the bar, the tequila untouched. "Fifteen years is a long time to hold on to a dream. And now that I have it . . ." He gestured wordlessly, unwilling or unable to express the final truth.

"There's nothing left to hope for," she finished for him. He said nothing, but she knew that she had hit home. She sipped at her drink for a moment, sensing that he wanted to say more.

"It's not the same," he said, groping for the words. "The game . . . it's all I ever wanted, but—" He looked up sharply, his blue eyes trained on hers as if daring her to contradict him. "I'm not a kid anymore," he added almost defiantly. "And—it's not enough."

Selena nodded thoughtfully, watching him. "There's always something more, around the bend," she murmured. "There's always something else to want, something else to strive for. Your dream was the dream of a twenty-year-old kid. But fifteen years went by, and that twenty-year-old kid is gone. Now you're left with the dream hanging around your neck, and you've outgrown it. You want more."

His eyes flooded with relief. "You understand," he said wonderingly.

"Of course I do," she said, surprised.

"I—I thought you might laugh at me. Or think I was the most selfish brute who ever lived."

She yearned to touch him, suddenly, to reach out and break the barrier between them forever. A tingling began in her fingertips, and she twisted her hands together unconsciously. "You're still chairman of the board and CEO of Derringer Industries," she reminded him playfully. But her tone became serious as she added, "And a very good one, at that."

He nodded. "You don't mind that?" He looked at her for a reaction, and she shook her head decisively. "I was good, but you're better," she said bluntly. "You were right, Trader. Paper boxes weren't for me." She watched as a smile began in the corners of his eyes. "But you have a knack for it. And I think it makes you happy," she added perceptively. "It's not football, but it's just as exciting in its own way—because you make it that way." The tingling had increased, spreading up her arms and into her throat, but still she held back.

Trader smiled at her, a real smile, and nodded. "We can run it together," he said eagerly. But the smile faded as she shook her head again.

"No," she said. "It wasn't my niche, and I'm not going back. You taught me that, you know."

"Oh." He looked so disappointed that her heart swelled, and the tingling danced all through her upper body. "What are you going to do?" he asked curiously.

Selena was waiting for that question. She dug into her purse and drew out a silver tie clip in the shape of a football. She pressed it into his palm and folded his fingers around it. "For you," she said. "One of the first designs of my new company—Derringer Jewelry Design." He looked surprised enough to fall off the stool, but he listened gamely as she explained. "I've already spoken to Henry about it. I'm going to sell off most of my remaining shares in Derringer to finance it. I'll still have a toehold in my father's company, but that's all."

His eyes widened. "You trust me?" he asked directly.

She didn't really have to answer, but she nodded gently, her eyes capturing his. The tingling had spread all through her body now, and she reached out at last, like a drowning man reaching for a life raft, to take his hand in hers.

Something snapped in his face and he took her other hand in his. "How do you do it?" he whispered. "How can you know me so well? I walked in here thinking I had lost everything, and now..." He left the thought unspoken, but she picked it up.

"You never lost, Trader," she said. "You never lost anything in your life. You got your season in the sun, you've got a company that needs you and makes you happy, and..." She took a deep breath and said it. "You've got me."

"Do I, Selena?" His face was filled with emotion, and she nodded tremulously. "Then I *have* won, because I love you. There's been a lot of give and take, hasn't there?" he asked gravely. "But it's all evened out in the end."

"That's the way it works," she whispered. "Not in football, maybe, but—"

"In love," he finished for her. "Do you love me, Selena?"

She gave a breathless little laugh. "Do you really have to ask? You know I do," she answered. "I've loved you inside for so long that it's built up like a flower about to burst into bloom."

He took her into his arms, his face riveting hers with a heart-stopping look of love. "I'll never stop loving you," he vowed, his brilliant blue eyes caressing her face. "You've been one hell of an adversary," he added wryly as he brought his head down to hers for a kiss that she knew would fulfill her and complete their union. "But from now on we're playing on the same team."

COMING NEXT MONTH
IN THE
SECOND CHANCE AT LOVE SERIES

SECOND CHANCE AT LOVE

Be Sure to Read These New Releases!

HEARTS ARE WILD #298 by Janet Gray
High-stakes poker player Emily Farrell never
loses her cool and *never* gambles on love—until alluring
Michael Mategna rips away her aloof façade and exposes
her soft, womanly yearnings.

SPRING MADNESS #299 by Aimée Duvall
The airwaves sizzle when zany deejay Meg
Randall and steamy station owner Kyle Rager join
forces to beat the competition...and end up
madly wooing each other.

SIREN'S SONG #300 by Linda Barlow
Is Cat MacFarlane a simple singer or a criminal
accomplice? Is Rob Hepburn a UFO investigator or
the roguish descendant of a Scots warrior clan? Their
suspicions entangle them in intrigue...and passion!

MAN OF HER DREAMS #301 by Katherine Granger
Jessie Dillon's looking for her one true love—and
she's sure Jake McGuire isn't it! How can a devious
scoundrel in purple sneakers who inspires such
toe-tingling lust possibly be the man of her dreams?

UNSPOKEN LONGINGS #302 by Dana Daniels
Joel Easterwood is a friend when Lesley Evans
needs one most. But she's secretly loved him since
childhood, and his intimate ministrations are
tearing her apart!

THIS SHINING HOUR #303 by Antonia Tyler
Kent Sawyer's blindness hasn't diminished his
amazing self-reliance...or breathtaking sexual appeal.
But is Eden Fairchild brave enough to allow this
extraordinary man to care for *her*?

Order on opposite page